Foreword

We are delighted to contribute this foreword to Beyond the Bookshelves by Ink Tank Creative Writing Group.

As we approach our 32nd Anniversary, Newbridge Samaritans is going from strength to strength.
We have in excess of 80 volunteers who take 2700 calls every month which equates to over 400 hours on the phones.
Without the support of our dedicated volunteers and our supporters in the local community, we would struggle to provide such a service.
Our branch also provides support to the Prison Service, and we provide listening services at festivals such as Electric Picnic, Dublin Pride, etc.
We also reach out to schools and introduce our services to the students.

We would like to take this opportunity to thank you for your support.

Judy Murphy
Newbridge Director.

SAMARITANS
Newbridge & Kildare

Copyright © 2024 Ink Tank Creative Writing Group

The right of Ink Tank Creative Writing Group to be identified as the Author of the Work has been asserted by them in accordance with the Copyright, Designs and Patents Act 1988.

First published in 2024 by Ink Tank Creative Writing Group.

Apart from any use permitted under UK copyright law, this publication may only be reproduced, stored, or transmitted, in any form, or by any means, with prior permission in writing of the publisher or, in the case of reprographic production, in accordance with the terms of licences issued by the Copyright Licensing Agency. All characters in this publication are fictitious and any resemblance to real persons, living or dead, is purely coincidental.

Print ISBN: 9798879212037

Behind the Bookshelves

Ink Tank Creative Writers Group

What happens when a small-town
writing group is taken hostage
in their local library?

Lives will be threatened,
and mayhem will ensue.

Will anyone survive unscathed?

Read on to find out...

Chapter 1

A scream tore through the hushed silence of the library, echoed by a shriek from Sadie, the youngest of the writing group.

"Sorry, I got such a fright there, you know how jumpy I can be," she said, as the scribbling ceased around the table.

"That sounds like someone is in trouble. I think we should investigate. If nothing else, it will be a good prompt for our next writing session," said Maxwell, in a voice raspy from excessive cigarettes.

"It certainly warrants investigation but please Maxwell, be careful." Siobhan spoke with the quiet authority gained from years of teaching science to teenagers. With a collective scraping of fold-out metal chairs, the group of five made for the door. There was the usual fiddling and fuzzing with the magnetic locking system on the door. Having conquered this, Maxwell led the way out into the hall.

"I'll just pop into the loo," said Olive in her quiet voice as she slipped away from the back of the group. Oblivious, Maxwell marched out into the library. Arthritis had taken its toll on his elderly joints, but he still managed to keep an upright stance. Before he could lead the group around the corner and into the library proper, Siobhan's gentle but firm hand grasped Maxwell's arm, stopping him.

"Listen," Siobhan hissed, still holding firmly onto Maxwell.

Muffled by the shelves of books, the group could hear sobs and laboured breathing from the reception desk area.

"Shut up. I'll stab you if you don't stop.'

The voice sounded unnaturally loud in the usual tranquillity of the library and was reinforced with another scream. The raw terror in the scream caused the group to flinch back into the alcove of the books. The inconsolable whimpering and sobbing that followed the scream caused the fight or flight reaction of the male ego to kick in.

"I'll hop out the window and get help," Daniel whispered and retreated into the writing room.

On the other hand, Maxwell, muttering nonsense, straightened his back, shook off Siobhan and rounded the corner.

"What is the meaning of this?" said Maxwell as he strode to the front desk.

Sheer stubbornness was the only thing that kept his feet moving as he took in the scene in front of him. A man that Maxwell could only have described as a thug stood at the main desk. A shirt had certainly never graced this man's back. He had dragged the poor librarian halfway across the countertop by her blouse and was waving a wicked-looking knife. Without a word, he dropped the poor unfortunate woman and swung a meaty fist into Maxwell's face. Maxwell felt a sickly pop as his nose gave way to the man's fist. This was quickly followed by searing pain and gushing blood. His vision blurred as the momentum of the blow toppled him to the floor in a pile. A second, slightly older thug stepped forward and leaned over Maxwell.

"Where did you come from? Are there any more of you hiding back there?"

Maxwell moaned as his shaking hands went in search of his ruined nose.

"For fuck's sake, JJ, you clocked him too hard. He can't answer me. Just go find out yourself," the older thug said.

Siobhan held up her hands as JJ rushed around the corner.

"Don't hurt us. It's just us. We'll do whatever you want."

"Fuck. There's more of them, Larry. What should I do?" JJ called back over his shoulder.

"Get them out here where we can see them," Larry replied.

"You heard him, move it," said JJ.

The whimpering of the librarian and Maxwell's groans were enough of an incentive for the group of three women to move quickly, but JJ wasn't happy. He grabbed Siobhan's arm, shoving her further.

"Son, would you manhandle your own mother like this?" Siobhan asked looking unflinchingly at the young man. JJ grunted, but he let go of her arm.

In the main room, Larry had moved the librarian from behind the desk but had a fist full of her blouse.

"Right, everyone face down on the floor, if you don't want to get hurt," Larry said.

"Young man, I am too old for that. Surely, I can just take a seat here." Siobhan said.

"You can get down yourself, or I'll knock you down. I don't think you will take that any better than Pops over there," Larry said.

Siobhan eased herself to the floor. The librarian started to drop to her knees, but Larry pulled her back up.

"Not you. You're going to help me lock up," said Larry, "JJ watch these."

Everyone else joined Maxwell on the worn short-haired carpet as the security cage, and then the library's front doors were closed and locked. Maxwell was still a spluttering mess with blood flowing freely. His laboured breathing was spraying blood into the air and on the ground around him.

"Face down means on your belly Pops. Roll over before I hit you again," JJ growled.

Maxwell was oblivious to the renewed threat. When his brain ignored the pain long enough to operate, he was filled with thoughts of disbelief. When had he stopped being able to take a punch? Sweet lord, had it always hurt this much?

Before JJ could make good on his threat, Larry returned and shoved the librarian to the ground.

"Betty here tells me there is another door out that way," said Larry nodding his head at the fire door in the opposite direction from where the writing group had emerged.

"We need to get this place locked down. Give me your gun while I go sort it out," said Larry.

Still waving the knife JJ removed a sleek black handgun from the waistband of his tracksuit bottoms. Larry quickly slipped the gun into the pocket of his grey zip-up hoodie. Now that the group on the floor had seen him put it there, the weapon was easily recognisable in his pocket. They wouldn't be forgetting about it anytime soon.

"You in the pink, get up and help me find these doors," said Larry. "And you, stop that crying, or I will put a bullet in you."

"Why are you taking the hot one with you and leaving me the cranks? What are you planning for back there?" said JJ.

"Focus JJ, there will be time enough for that once this place is locked down."

Sadie struggled to her feet with as much dignity as she could muster as the two men leered. Today wasn't the day for heels and a mini skirt, she thought, why didn't I wear my skinny jeans. But dignity was key, and she held her head up high as she led the way to the door, knowing full well Larry was behind her, enjoying the view.

The door swung closed behind them, and the group's attention snapped back to Maxwell. His coughing and spluttering were now drowning out the librarian's sobs as he struggled to breathe.

"Please let me help him," said Siobhan. She knew that if Maxwell didn't roll over soon, he might drown himself.

"No, don't you move. Nobody moves."

"We have to do something," pleaded Siobhan. "He can't breathe".

"Move, and you will be bleeding too," warned JJ in a snarl.

Maxwell's struggling increased as less air got past his blocked windpipe and into his burning lungs. He desperately clutched at his face and neck but remained on his back like a beached turtle.

"Please, let me help him. I know you don't want him to die." Siobhan tried again, but JJ was unmoved.

Chapter 2

Olive waited in the bathroom for the count of five agonisingly slow seconds, but she made herself count slowly Mississippi's and all. Then she cracked the bathroom door open again to an empty hall. She slipped out, and quickly collected her handbag. The size of a standard backpack, her handbag carried all her essentials and quite a number of non-essentials. Rummaging with one hand, she set off at a half trot along the corridor running behind the main library.

There had been a sense of terror in that scream they had heard, and she wasn't about to run straight at it like some greenhorn. Memory fades with age, but some lessons are bone-deep and are never forgotten. Moving as quietly as she could in her sensible shoes, Olive's hand pushed at an endless supply of tissues and pens in her bag in search of her phone.

Her hand brushed against something that had the right cool metallic plastic feel, but when her fist closed around it, it was too long and narrow to be her phone. Something for later, perhaps, but only as a last resort.

With frustration building, Olive was about to dump the bag out on the floor when she finally grasped her phone. Even in these precarious circumstances, she made a mental note that it was time for the annual handbag clear out. Olive slowed as her target came into sight. The door into the main library was on the other side from where her writing group had entered the building when they arrived earlier. She could hear aggressive shouting, but the heavy fire door was muffling the words. Knees creaking, Olive dropped down to a crawl and moved to the door, making sure she was well below the windowpane in the door, she moved with ease, her love of Pilates paying off. Her knees did creak, but sure they have done that since her twenties and had never held her back.

Putting her shoulder to the door, she pushed against it. Nothing happened. Fire doors are heavy. Pushing harder, the door moved, but her stomach muscles also made their presence known. 'No pain, no gain', isn't that what her godson also says. What a nuisance, but perhaps, in this case, true.

As the door eased open, Olive could clearly hear unfamiliar voices, and they were not happy. Risking a quick glance, she poked her head around the bottom of the door. Olive took in the scene; Maxwell, bloody on the floor and the rest of the writing group being herded by two men. Olive had seen enough, and she ducked back behind the door, letting it close. Only at the last minute did her instincts kick in and she put out a hand to slow the door as it closed.

Crawling away from the door she got to her feet. Heading back towards the bathroom she opened the first door she came to and went in. She unlocked her phone and started dialling as she took in the features of the room she had entered. It was part storage area, part office. Hopefully the piles of books and papers would dampen her voice.

Her phone dialled out twice before an impatient voice barked out of the speaker.

"Detective Chief Inspector Darcy speaking"

"Ciaran, it's me, Olive. Do you not have my number saved? Why are you detective chief Inspecting me?"

"Oh yea, sorry Olive, just a habit. Olive this is not a great time to talk. Can I call you back later?" he said rather sheepishly.

"I'm in the library."

"Wait, you're in the library? Newbridge Library?"

"Yes."

"What's happening, say more."

Those two similar words 'say more' triggered a mental reflex for Olive and she began speaking quietly.

'Two hostiles, possibly armed, entered the library and appear to have taken four hostages, the librarian and three from the writing group. Unknown if there are other hostages, possibly one guy."

"Copy Olive. Sit tight and do nothing. We will be there soon," said Ciaran. A blast from the Garda siren followed Ciaran's voice down the phone.

Olive tried to get hold of the conversation.

"Hold on a minute Ciaran, you are already outside, I can hear you. And how did you know there was something going on in the library and know enough in advance to already be here? I don't denigrate the Gardai, but your response times are not that good, especially to launch your unit.'

"We got a tip off that something was going on. And before you say it, it was from a source that we don't ignore. We had hoped to get there sooner but the Irish Derby means those damn racehorse nerds and gamblers have clogged up Newbridge. Look I got to go. If you can get out safely do that, otherwise sit tight. But no heroics, leave that to the professionals."

"Okay, but why the hell are they in the library? They're not here to steal books, and I know for sure there are no celebrities here."

"We haven't figured that out yet. But we think these are big players, and dangerous. So, no heroics, promise me."

"Okay."

"Olive don't okay me. I know you well. You have had a very tough time but don't give up on me. Think of your husband, think of your godson, think of me and the guilt you will lay on me if anything bad happens to you. I know you better than that quiet gentle grandmother veneer you show people, but I also know the type of dangerous criminal you have in there. So, promise me you won't do anything I will regret. Stay safe and let me do my job."

"Okay, I promise, I won't do anything you will regret."

"The dead have no regrets." They both said in union.

"Ok, I got to go. Stay safe."

Olive stood looking at her phone as the call ended. She knew there was a lot that Ciaran hadn't told her, but what could she expect, he had a job to do. The mantra of an earlier life was ringing in her ears as Olive slipped back of into the hall. Turning her head, she looked up and down the hall, left at the potentially open exit and out to Ciaran and then right which led back to the bathroom to sit in the middle of the chaos. Her blood was up, and adrenaline was pumping, so there was no question, right it was. She had promised Ciaran, but he had said sit tight and that was what she would do. Back to the bathroom and sit tight. They say a man on the inside might turn the tide in events, but no one ever mentions the impact a kindly grandmother on the inside might have on events. Time to find out.

Chapter 3

Sadie wobbled out the fire doors in front of Larry. Fear turned her long legs to jelly as she stumbled along like a toddler in her mother's new shoes. To her right was a large glass door with two side panels, the glass interwoven with steel security mesh. Sadie gasped at the spectacle outside the doors. Sirens filled the air overriding the shouts of the gardai. She spotted armed Gardai, their guns trained on the library. Sadie hesitated, not sure which way to turn.

"Move."

Larry shoved Sadie with the palm of his hand between her shoulder blades, and she stumbled towards an alcove on the far side of the outer doors.

"Ouch." Sadie felt her ankle twist in her unsuitable footwear, causing her to fall, landing heavily on her knees.

"Shit! Get up, for fucks sake."

"I've twisted my ankle." Sadie croaked.

"Shit, shit, shit. That's all I fucking need." Larry's voice was a low growl.

Sadie flashed a look of pure anger at her aggressor but thought better of answering him. She pulled off her shoes and hauled herself upright, holding onto the wall for support. Tears threatened to overwhelm her, the initial flash of anger superseded by fear.

Larry ignored her as he stared at the scene outside, deep in thought. She took a long, hard look at him. He couldn't be much older than thirty, she reckoned. His lower face was covered by a black fabric mask that hid his jawline. Above the mask, his eyes were a piercing sea blue, large for his face and framed with thick dark lashes that any woman would envy. His unruly dark brown hair desperately needed a good cut but was obviously recently washed with a citrus shampoo. An athletic frame suggested a runner, which led her to wonder how far she could get if she made a run for the door.

"Get over there and bolt that door."

Larry's words shook her out of her reverie. She limped over, wincing with the pain in her left ankle as terror took hold of her. Would the armed Gardai outside presume she was one of them and open fire on her? Trembling, she checked the lock then pulled across the bolts at the top and the bottom of the door.

"Close the blinds."

Larry took the gun out of his pocket slowly, holding it pointed downward like an extension of his hand, his manicured forefinger sliding along the shiny surface. Sadie stared in horror at his long fingers, unblemished by hard work. The hands of a pianist, she thought.

"The blinds," he growled at her. As slowly as she could manage, Sadie did as she was told, silently willing the Garda outside to storm the building, and set them free.

"Any other exits?"

Fear stole her voice from her. She opened her mouth to answer, but no words came out. That frightened her even more. It was like the bad dreams she had as a teenager. Dreams where she was in danger, but her voice wouldn't work. Her mother always woke her from those dreams, holding her and telling her that everything was okay. A sob escaped her as the longing for the comfort of her mother's arms swept through her.

Larry clicked his tongue, shaking his head, leaving Sadie in no doubt that he was losing patience with her.

"I...I...don't know, I usually go out this door," Sadie said.

Larry flashed her a look that suggested he considered her an idiot, and Sadie backed away. She could feel beads of sweat running down her back under her pink top and cursed herself again for her choice of outfit. It was a last-minute decision. The bedroom chair that her mother laughingly called her wardrobe was full of clothes. Her skinny jeans and blue sweatshirt had been on top of the pile, but she had moved them aside to pick out this stupid mini skirt and pale, pink top. What was she thinking? It was hardly an appropriate outfit for a meeting of the sedate writers group. Sadie gulped, trying to fold her arms around herself like some self-conscious teenager.

His derisory laugh startled her.

"Get back to the others, you silly cow."

He waved the gun at her, gesturing back towards the others. With a sigh of relief, Sadie turned and limped, barefoot, back to the main room. Maxwell was still choking while JJ continued to shout at the others to shut up.

"Get over there with the rest of them."

Larry used the gun to point to where the others lay on the floor, but Sadie couldn't pass Maxwell. Her Order of Malta training kicked in. Without stopping to think, she knelt and pushed Maxwell over onto his side, oblivious of JJ's roars to stop. Siobhan leapt to help her, and between them, they got Maxwell into the recovery position.

"What the fuck do you think you're doing?" JJ stormed over and slapped Sadie hard across the head, knocking her into Siobhan, and they both sprawled on the floor.

"For goodness' sake, there is no need for gratuitous violence," Siobhan said.

"Shut up, do ye hear me, shut – the – fuck – up," JJ emphasised each word with a fist on the counter.

That's enough, JJ," Larry said, "Between them wittering and you roaring, I can't hear myself think."

Sadie sobbed quietly, deep intakes of breath that threatened to choke her. Siobhan held her tight, trying to comfort her, until gradually her breathing returned to normal. Larry signalled to JJ to follow him, and as soon as they rounded the corner, Sadie and Siobhan went back to Maxwell's aid.

"What's happening outside?" Siobhan whispered.

Sadie glanced furtively towards the corner bookshelves where Larry and JJ were having some sort of heated yet whispered debate.

"Armed Garda, lots of them."

Betty crept behind the counter and returned in seconds with a first aid kit. Maxwell was looking better, if a shade puce, but at least he was breathing normally again. The shrill sound of the telephone brought JJ and Larry running to the centre of the library. Betty backed up against the counter, trembling, her eyes wide as sobs escaped her. Sadie took in her torn blouse and her increasing distress. Black trails of black mascara snaked down her cheeks as the volume of her sobs increased.

"Shut up," JJ roared at her as he paced up and down while the phone rang on and on. Betty's sobs died in her throat, leaving her a quivering mess. Then, as suddenly as it started, the phone stopped ringing, and JJ stopped pacing. Sadie's eyes were drawn to the vicious-looking knife he wielded in his right hand. JJ raised his left hand, pulled off his Ferrari baseball cap and scratched his dirty blond crew cut. Sadie looked closer, sensing something familiar about him.

Of course, the mask disguised most of his face, but with the cap removed, she realised she definitely knew him from somewhere. He had an oval face, no obvious beard, with fair eyebrows and a high forehead. There was a black earring in one ear and what she guessed could be the beginning of a tattoo peeking out from under his sweatshirt on his left.

Siobhan noticed her look of surprise and nudged her. Sadie shook her head, afraid to speak in the complete silence that surrounded them. Even the sirens outside had stopped. Sadie felt as if the world was holding its breath, waiting on JJ to react.

The tinny bellow of the loudspeaker startled them all.

"Attention, this is Detective Chief Inspector Darcy."

JJ put his cap back on and circled back to Larry, the knife held outward, threatening them. He moved like a boxer waiting on his opponent to make the first move. In that instant, Sadie realised who he was. She hadn't seen him in years, but she was sure it was John. His appearance had changed, and not for the better. His drug abuse showed in his eyes and in his steroid fuelled physique. The last time she saw him, he held the regional boxing title. There was even talk of him turning professional.

"Attention, inside the library. We have patched through the phones. Pick up, and let's talk."

All eyes turned to the reception counter where the streamlined cream coloured phone sat beside the computer monitor. There was a collective intake of breath when it rang. Larry stared at it for a beat, then sauntered over behind the counter and pulled over the librarian's leather swivel chair. The phone stopped ringing. Sadie and Siobhan exchanged worried glances. Maxwell tried to move, but Siobhan put her hand on his arm and her finger to her lips.

The phone rang again. Larry lifted the receiver on the second ring, lifted it to his ear but said nothing. The four women strained their ears. JJ hopped from one foot to the other.

"Safe passage Detective Chief Inspector. That should be easy for you to arrange."

Larry listened intently, then sighed.

"That's a no. The hostages stay inside until you deliver. You have two hours."

Larry replaced the receiver and stretched. He put his feet on the desk, his arms behind his head and yawned.

"Relax, ladies and gent. We're going to be here for a while. Get yourselves comfortable."

"What did he say, Larry," JJ asked.

"Later, JJ."

Larry got up from his relaxed position. "Right, you lot. Move. I want you all seated, backs against the reception desk where I can keep an eye on you."

"You heard him." JJ waved the knife at them.

Sadie and Siobhan helped Maxwell move across the floor and propped him against the reception desk, then sat on either side of him. Betty was in the same position, still hugging her knees to her chest and rocking slightly. Larry stood in front of them, his back to the public doors, now shuttered and locked.

"I don't want to harm any of you. But... I will if I have to."

He nodded at JJ, and the two of them disappeared around the corner of the bookshelves towards the staff corridor again.

Siobhan reached out and touched Betty's arm. She gasped loudly.

"What's going on?" Larry bounced up the steps and glowered at them.

Sadie rubbed her hand over her twisted ankle. "It's very painful; it's swollen. Look"

Larry looked at her with such disdain that Sadie cowered, pressing her back against the hard surface as if trying to disappear into it.

"Stay quiet. That goes for all of you."

Maxwell opened his mouth to speak, but Siobhan put a placating hand on his arm, shaking her head slightly.

"That's it, old man. Silence is golden." Larry glared at each of them in turn before turning back to the staff area. A fragile silence reigned for a minute until they were sure he was out of earshot. Sadie knelt in front of Betty and put her finger on her lips.

In a voice barely above a whisper, she asked, "Are all the exits locked?"

Betty nodded. "Everywhere is locked. I was waiting on you to leave to set the alarm when they burst in." She glanced at the direction Larry left, "but I think someone is in the public toilet. It was locked from the inside, but I pretended to lock it before he could try the door."

Sadie nodded. "Did they take the keys?"

Betty nodded, relaxing a little, much to Sadie's relief.

"But there's a spare set in my top drawer.

Chapter 4

Sergeant Moore frowned as his mobile phone buzzed in his breast pocket. Lifting out the mobile he glanced at the number and sighed. Not again.

"What?" His impatience evident in his curt tone. "Stop ringing me. I'm doing all I can."

He hung up, put the phone back in his pocket, then thought better of it. Taking it out, he turned it off completely. How did he get himself into this mess? Although he knew why. He could blame his wife and her expensive tastes but if he were to be totally honest with himself, he knew that if hadn't run up that gambling debt, they would never have found him.

Although, she never asked where the money came from. Surely, she realised that a Garda didn't earn the kind of money needed to fund their lifestyle. Did she really believe he earned that kind of money gambling? His mates, or rather his work colleagues for he had no friends, thought the money came from his wife. He never let anyone get close. How could he? If anyone even suspected what he was up to, he would be locked up. He had hinted at that enough times, had joked about how he had married well. In fairness, he thought he had. His wife was the only child of a doting father. Widowed now, but as mean as dishwater. They wouldn't be getting a cent until that ole fucker died and unfortunately, he was as fit as an ox.

Up until now it had been simple stuff. Pass on some information about Garda whereabouts, the odd tip on the movement of cash. It's amazing the number of wealthy people who ask the Gardai to keep an eye on their homes when they're away. He rarely felt any guilt over passing on that type of information. The targets were carefully chosen; only those who could afford it. If they lost cash or jewellery, they were well insured. And he had very little sympathy for insurance companies.

This job was different though. For a start it was worth a cool ten grand. Enough to get him out of yet another financial black hole. His lucky streak ran out during the Irish Oaks. But for the first time he was nervous about it. Up until now the information he had fed back was innocuous. This time felt different. Even though nothing had been said, it was the first time he had been told what to do, rather than just pass on relevant information. His gut clenched and a bead of sweat ran down his back.

He could no longer kid himself that he wasn't doing anything wrong. The ten grand in cash hidden in the boot of his car was proof that he was crooked. He had been sucked in slowly. He needed to get out, maybe consider early retirement. They had that holiday apartment in Alicante. He fancied life in the sun. A slower pace, sangria and siesta in the afternoon. He could even set up a security company, but he would need to move quickly. As soon as this job was over. Before he got caught. All he had to do was persuade his wife.

Chapter 5

"What did I tell you?" JJ roared and pushed Sadie onto her side. "Sit with your back against that counter and don't move. Do ye hear me?"

Sadie yelped as she scampered back into position in between Betty and Maxwell. Betty reached out to her and rubbed her arm while Siobhan squeezed her hand in silent support.

"There's no need to be so rough with her," Siobhan said. "She's only trying to help."

JJ scowled at her. "Shut the fuck up or you'll be next."

Siobhan visibly shrank away from him, pressing her back to the counter as if she were trying to weld herself into it. Siobhan could feel Sadie's body trembling beside her and squeezed her hand again, trying to comfort her while her own thoughts raced, trying to make sense of what was happening around her. Who would believe that anyone could be taken hostage in a library of all places? What could these men possibly want? There's no fine art or collector's items on display, nothing worth stealing, certainly nothing worth taking hostages for. Just thousands of bog-standard books in a bog-standard library, like thousands of libraries up and down the country.

The older one, Larry, had asked for safe passage. That much she had heard during that one-way telephone conversation. Were they chased in here while they were running away from a robbery? Larry carried a Northface backpack that looked fairly heavy, and he seemed to be protective of it. He hadn't taken it off at all, even when he was pretending to be so relaxed on the phone. Siobhan watched as Larry signalled to JJ and they disappeared down the staff corridor again.

"We have to get out of here," Siobhan said. Sadie was surprised to hear the steely determination in Siobhan's voice. "There's four of us," Siobhan said. "We could try and overpower them."

"Look how that worked out for poor Maxwell," Sadie said.

Betty spoke up, "There's a fire exit in the corridor over at the staff entrance. It's a push bar mechanism, no lock. It was only fitted yesterday."

"What are we waiting for," Maxwell said as he attempted to stand up just as JJ came back into the room.

Where do you think you're going?" JJ roared. "Sit the fuck down."

JJ held a coil of rope which he shook in Maxwell's direction as if to threaten to beat him with it. Maxwell collapsed back against the counter and Siobhan helped him to the ground, much to JJ's amusement. Siobhan watched as JJ returned to his task. Sadie tugged her hand and whispered, "If I create a diversion, you make a run for it. Get help."

Siobhan nodded.

"I'll stay here with Maxwell," Betty whispered. "You've a better chance with just two. Get some help as quick as you can."

JJ whistled as he worked. He dropped the rope at the front door and selected one long piece. Feeding the rope through the door handles he secured it with cable ties.

"Best little invention ever," he grinned. "A multitude of uses."

Siobhan and Sadie exchanged glances. If Siobhan was going to attempt to get out that fire exit, she was going to need that diversion quickly. JJ moved to the door leading out to the staff entrance. Without warning, Sadie jumped to her feet and ran towards JJ. She hit him with such force she knocked him off his feet and jumped on top of him.

"Run," she shouted while plummeting JJ with her fists.

Siobhan jumped to her feet and ran for the door. She flung it open. The fire exit was fifty feet away, the plaster around its frame still damp. Siobhan sprinted, reached out and pushed the bar, expecting it to release automatically. It brought her to a grinding halt. Nothing happened. Siobhan could feel panic rising in her chest as she pushed the quick release handle again. That panic turned to fear as she felt her hair tugged from behind.

"Leaving us, are you?" JJ released his grip on her hair and grabbed her arm, shaking her like a rag doll in the process. Suddenly Sadie was on his back, biting and thumping, JJ roared as he tried to shake her off, but she was like something possessed. Letting go of Siobhan he backed forcefully into the wall, winding Sadie and she fell to the ground. Siobhan ran to help but met the palm of JJ's hand straight into her chest. She fell beside Sadie, struggling for breath.

"You shouldn't have done that. Do you hear me? You shouldn't have done that. Now look at you. I don't want to hurt you. Do you hear me? I don't want too but God help me if I have to I will."

JJ's voice shook, whether with fear or rage, Siobhan wasn't sure. The one thing she was sure of was, she wasn't going to attempt to escape again in a hurry. In front of her JJ stood, bent over, with his hands on his knees, taking deep breaths. Siobhan didn't know why they had been taken hostage. She no longer cared. All she wanted was to get out of there, in one piece.

Larry appeared in the doorway. He reached down, grabbed her by the arm and pulled her to her feet.

"You too," he said as JJ dragged Sadie to a standing position. "No more, do you hear me, both of ye. If you just sit, be quiet, we'll be out of here in no time. Okay?"

He looked at them both, waiting for an answer. Siobhan nodded reluctantly, still reeling from the thump to her chest. Sadie flashed him a look of pure hatred and for a second Siobhan thought she was considering spitting in his face. Larry waited expectantly until Sadie eventually nodded her head. He led them back to the others, first Larry with a firm hold on Siobhan's right arm, then JJ, struggling to contain a squirming Sadie.

"Don't hurt her," Siobhan said, reaching out to take Sadie's hand. Larry dragged her away and pushed her roughly onto the ground beside Maxwell. JJ dragged Sadie by her hair and flung her down in front of them.

Larry stood in front of them, brandishing the gun.

"Stay quiet, stay still and you won't get hurt."

He nodded at JJ, who grinned and returned to his tasks, reinforcing the locks on the staff entrance.

"Make sure you secure that fire exit," Larry said. JJ nodded and commenced whistling. The sound followed them back to the main library, the happy tune at odds with the tension pulsating in the room.

Chapter 6

Thirty minutes had passed since Larry gave Detective Inspector Darcy two hours to arrange safe passage for him and JJ out of the library. Betty stole a glance each side of her. Since the failed escape attempt, they were kept lined up, nervously sitting with their backs to the reception desk. Siobhan sent glances and whispers of reassurance to the group, which was somewhat comforting although Sadie seemed oblivious, nursing her sore ankle and exuding visible anger towards her captors.

Betty had regained her composure after her encounter with JJ when he grabbed and tore her blouse as he roared at her. She had always been shy, soft spoken yet highly strung. The quiet, organised life of a librarian suited her. There was nothing to fear, other than what lay between the pages of the crime thrillers she indulged in. But today she had experienced real fear. Those two men had appeared out of nowhere, just as she was about to lock up for the evening. She had never felt so threatened but now she had a chance to study them there was something about the older one. His eyes were familiar and for some unknown reason she thought of Jack Fitzgerald.

Seated on the floor next to Siobhan and Sadie, Betty tucked her torn blouse into her bra strap and pulled her long billowy skirt around her legs. She made herself as comfortable as possible, her thoughts turning to her mother who had grown to depend on Betty since her husband died.

Betty was an only child and never married. She was shy and introverted growing up, with just a few friends. Betty loved school and books. On the weekends she didn't hang out with her school friends. She was content to stay home and read which avoided fifty questions from her controlling mother.

At sixteen she was encouraged by her parents to attend the Christmas school dance. It was chaperoned by the nuns and brothers. For the first time Betty danced with a boy who attended the brother's secondary school.

Jack Fitzgerald was a year older than Betty; he was 6ft 2ins tall and built like an athlete. His dark hair and hazel eyes made him the most handsome man she had ever met. Betty was enamoured by the attention he bestowed on her, and they danced happily together. He had a kind heart, and a calm demeanour. As the night wore on Betty was smitten. Her feelings were unprecedented, and she liked being the centre of Jack's attention. They met after school and at least once on the weekends. When they left school to attend two different colleges, they kept their relationship alive with phone calls during the week and visits when Jack made it home two weekends a month.

When Betty was eighteen her father died. It was Jack who comforted her. She dared not seek comfort from her mother, who was too consumed in her own grief and self-pity to consider her daughters feelings. Betty and Jack had never been intimate, but that changed. Three months after her father's funeral, Betty told Jack she was pregnant. Feeling her mother would be less than supportive, they decided to put the child, a boy, up for adoption. The decision broke both their hearts. At eighteen and nineteen they knew they couldn't raise a child. After their son was born, the strain of it all forced them to go their separate ways. Betty finished college and weeks later she secured a position at the local library. Jack entered the seminary and became a priest.

Living with her mother all these years had been safe, although Betty knew she was hiding herself and her secret from the world as much as from her mother. She felt shame and knew she could never tell her mother as she would never forgive her for having a child out of wedlock. The guilt of giving him up for adoption played a huge part in her secluded life and mind. She often told herself she didn't deserve anything more from life.

Betty was now fifty-one years old. Her mother was eighty and depended on her daughter more than ever. Betty contemplated giving up her position at the library to care for her ailing mother full time. However, her mother talked her out of it. Betty had always been a home bird; never lived away from home, never been outside Ireland. As an adult she saw less of the few friends she had. Even her holidays from the library were spent with her mother, visiting family in Galway.

Betty's discovery of books and the solitude of libraries from a young age helped her decide being a librarian was the career for her. After college and with a degree in Social Studies, Betty took a course to get a qualification in library and information science. The rest was history.

As her mother became more infirm, she insisted a home help was all she needed until Betty got home from work. The home help left just fifteen minutes before Betty was due in from work. Her mother insisted she could manage on her own for short periods.

Today was going to be different. Betty was fretting as she was unable to contact home. She wanted to ask her mother's assistant to stay. She worried about the evening meal and the medication her mother depended on. This made Betty angrier at her captors.

Chapter 7

Angela tutted to herself as she checked the kitchen clock again. Her programme was about to start and here she was, settled in her usual chair but with no cup of tea. Betty was never home late. You could set your clock by her daughter, so regular was she in her routines, a real creature of habit. But then so was Angela and this creature of habit needed her evening cup of tea.

As the time passed, Angela's irritation began to give way to concern. What was keeping Betty? Angela leaned over to pick up her mobile phone from the end table and tried again to call Betty, but with no success. Her phone was turned off. Angela had thought of calling the library, but her memory wasn't what it used to be. She couldn't recall the number. Angela didn't return the phone to the table but held it on her lap, turning it over anxiously in her hands.

She didn't like this phone as much as her last one. It seemed to her that this one was quieter, harder to hear the caller. She was getting more nuisance calls recently too. She couldn't really blame the new mobile for that, but she was a believer in not fixing what wasn't broken. Her neighbour had given her the new phone. He was trying to be kind. He told her it would be easier for her to use. Her eyesight wasn't strong anymore and she struggled to read the screen. This new phone had no buttons but a big square when you woke it up that she could press to call Betty. She didn't even need to key in the numbers. Which meant she was forgetting phone numbers. Which meant she couldn't remember the library's number.

Which meant she couldn't check if Betty was still at her desk. Angela sighed and replaced the useless phone, cursing her neighbour's misguided kindness and saying a silent prayer that Betty would be back soon. Her programme had started but she hadn't noticed.

Chapter 8

Larry paced the length of the main library as the minutes ticked by. He tried to keep his mind on the situation at hand. All the while hoping the Detective Inspector would value the lives of the hostages and arrange safe passage for him and JJ.

Something in Larry's heart made him feel guilty for shouting and grabbing this gentle soul, it wasn't her fault that he and JJ had taken cover in her library. That damned brother of mine, he thought. If only he hadn't got mixed up with the wrong crowd. Larry was shocked when his twenty-five-year-old brother, Ben, approached him for his help.

Despite the age difference, Larry and Ben were buddies growing up, being the older brother Ben often copied his every move and word. As a teenager Larry got into many scrapes in school and during after-school activities, nothing too serious but enough to warrant his parents disapproval. He had always felt a little left out of the family, like something was missing; he felt an allegiance had to be proved in order to be accepted.

Whereas Ben got out of control at a much younger age, committing petty theft and often turning to Larry for help before the Gardai or his parents found out. Their father blamed Larry for leading poor Ben astray. Something that left Larry feeling even more disconnected from the family.

Marie was his saving grace. It was love at first sight for Larry. She was everything he ever wanted. He felt a connection to Marie that he had never experienced before. It was Marie that encouraged him to go for the job in the bookies. He had always been on the other side of the counter, winning more than he lost overall. When Charlie approached him and offered him the job doing the tote at race meetings around the country his first reaction was to laugh out loud. But Charlie was serious, and Marie thought it was a great idea. Six months later Charlie offered him the manager's job in the bookie shop. It was a dream come true. Full time employment. A steady wage. He could plan for the future, a future with Marie.

Larry sank into the chair with his head in his hands as wave after wave of despair hit him. His whole future was now at risk, thanks to little brother. The most recent confession from Ben was that he was into a drug deal for a large sum of money. Larry couldn't believe what he was hearing. Petty theft was bad enough but drugs. His fists still itched to knock some sense into his brother.

Not that he got the chance. That phone call changed everything. Larry didn't know where they were holding Ben. All they said was that unless Larry did exactly what they told him to do, they would kill his brother. What choice did he have?

That disembodied voice on his mobile haunted him.

"It's simple, Larry. All you have to do is let my pal rob your bookie shop. Let him walk away with a rucksack full of cash. Once I get the cash, you get your brother."

"But..."

"It's not open for debate, Larry. Listen, be a good brother. Give my pal the cash. I give you your brother. His debt wiped clean."

Somewhere niggling at the back of his mind Larry thought that maybe, just maybe, today would be the day his parents would praise him for getting his brother out of trouble. Maybe they would see the true Larry and love him as much as they loved Ben. Another sound from the corridor bolted Larry out of absorption of his past.

"What was that? Did you hear a noise from here JJ?"

"Hell no," JJ replied. Larry and JJ without giving a thought to their hostages raced to the corridor and stood listening.

"There, did you hear that?" Larry muttered.

"No man, you're getting paranoid," JJ responded as he strolled back to take his position guarding the group.

"I'm not frigging paranoid, you idiot, there's someone else in the building."

Larry quickly walked back to reception breaking the petrified silence of the group.

"Who is missing? And don't bloody lie, I'm not a fool." He pointed to Siobhan.

"You, who else is here?" he said in a rough manner even with his cultured accent.

Siobhan reluctantly replied, "I don't know, I can't remember how many of us were in the room."

The group remained quiet as Larry and JJ strolled from their respective sides of the main reception. Changing places had put Larry nearer the corridor to the writing room, loo, and back rooms.

JJ demanded to know who was hiding. He turned on Siobhan using the butt of the gun to get her attention. She recoiled in horror as if stuck in a nightmare, unable to move from the horrific memories of past abuse.

"Who is missing," Larry shouted causing her to snap back to the present.

"We're all here," she whispered in a frightened voice, wondering if she would regret her lie.

"I just heard a noise and I think someone is hiding, so spill, you old biddy or else."

Siobhan was so nervous she couldn't take the risk of another lie.

"It may be Olive."

"Who the hell is Olive and where is she?" he shouted.

"Leave her alone," shouted Sadie.

Larry pointed the gun at her.

"Shut up, nobody asked you."

The group held their breath, waiting for her to answer.

"Find her and find her now. The noise came from out there." Larry bellowed at JJ as he pointed towards the corridor. JJ headed in the direction indicated.

"Wait, take this one with you," Larry grabbed Betty by the shoulder pulling her to her feet and pushed her towards JJ. "Use this one as bait, make her come out of hiding."

Pulling her torn blouse close to her body, Betty moved in front of JJ. She feared what they would do to Olive when they found her. Shouting her name as he went, JJ began to threaten harm to Betty and the group if she didn't show herself. As they neared the bathroom door Olive opened it, walking into the corridor hands held high, eyes closed, and her heart pounding in her chest.

JJ sprang into action, grabbed Olive's arm, pushed her towards the main reception, as he waved the knife to beckon Betty to follow suit.

"This is ridiculous," Larry threw his hands up in the air. "You're all too brave for my liking, JJ go find something to tie them. Hurry".

Olive sat next to Maxwell and Siobhan as silent tears streamed down her cheeks.

"It'll be ok," Sadie whispered.

JJ returned with a roll of duct tape, proud of his find in the plumbers' toolbox behind the utility room door. He extended the roll to Larry.

"What the hell man, can't you think for yourself? Tape their hands, fool."

Looking sheepish JJ began to tape Maxwell's hands.

"For Christ's sake can you not see he's injured and no threat," Sadie announced.

"Tape this bitch first, and her mouth too, if she doesn't shut it," Larry said.

One by one JJ taped their wrists, closely watched by Larry as he paced the floor showing signs of uneasiness. The phone rang, piercing through an already tense atmosphere where nerves were on a knife edge. Sadie was apprehensive to speak but had to find a reason to get JJ alone. He might re-think his role holding a fellow past classmate's sister hostage. Could she reason with him? Possibly but not in front of Larry, that much she knew.

Chapter 9

It was no accident that Maxwell Riordan led the charge into the main area of the library. He had a lot to prove to himself. Firstly, that he was no coward and secondly that he could show leadership in a time of crisis.

Both qualities had been put to the test at a stage in his career as manager of a large bank branch in Dublin. Sadly, he was found to be lacking in both. This was his chance to restore his self-esteem. It took about 20 seconds for him to realise how foolhardy he was when his face was burst open by a sledgehammer blow to his nose. He lay groaning in a bloody pool on the floor with his hands cupping the bulbous mess on his face.

It was impossible to stem the flow as blood gushed in every direction, through what was left of his silver hair and down the newly laundered stripped shirt and grey slacks he had carefully chosen for this evening's meeting. Pain seared through his 65-year-old body as he crashed to the floor, his arthritic joints taking a hammering. Blood seeped into his throat making him gag as he laboured for breath.

"I'm choking," he tried to say but heard only gurgling sounds. Then he heard a woman's voice, hopefully Siobhan's, pleading "let me help him.... don't want him to die."

This confirmed his fears that he was near the end. Time meant nothing as he drifted in and out of oblivion, gasping and gurgling. He thought he had arrived in the hereafter when he heard an angel's voice - or perhaps it was a young woman's voice with a Kildare accent.

"Ok Maxwell, you're going to have to let us roll you over and you'll be able to breathe better. Stay with us Maxwell, don't drift off. You're going to be all right once we get you off your back. That's it, you're doing great."

He wasn't dead. Vaguely aware of his surroundings, Maxwell surrendered to the two ladies who gently pushed him on to his side and into the recovery position. Gradually his breathing steadied, and he realised he was a hostage, injured and powerless but relieved that he was not going to die, yet. He had no concept of time but surrendered to being helped to sit against the reception desk and having his wrists tied.

***

There was no denying the seriousness of the hostage situation. This week's free writing session – which the writers enjoyed every week – had the title "An undesirable encounter". How apt was that, thought Siobhan, who had plenty to write on the subject before they were even taken hostage. Oh yes, she had plenty of real-life experience on that topic.

Siobhan was struggling with her ageing joints as she, along with the others, was forced to sit on the hard floor. She wondered how long they would be tied up. She needed something to distract her from the pains in her back and knees. She leaned over towards Maxwell who was propped next to her against the reception desk. His face was so puffed and purple around his eyes she wasn't sure, if he could see. Caked blood was smeared all over his face and hair. A whispered conversation took place between them.

"Are you OK, Maxwell? My God, they really busted your nose good and proper. You must be in agony."

"It probably looks worse that it is - broken for sure but Sadie plugged it, so it's stopped bleeding. She's a grand girl, full of gumption for someone so young and flighty looking. Only for her I might be a gonner."

"Nonsense, Maxwell. You're tougher than you think and, let's face it, you did take on those two galoots which was really very brave." This was the first time Maxwell had heard that said to him. He managed a smile.

***

Olive was ashen faced and shaken as she was manhandled into an uncomfortable position beside Maxwell on the ground. She looked around the room, horrified to see her lovely group tied up and so terrified. Looking to her left and was shocked to see the cut of Maxwell, felled and stripped of his dignity and, although sometimes she felt uncomfortable with his pompous manner, she hated to see him so humiliated.

"Why are we hostages, Maxwell?" she whispered. "God almighty, look at the cut of you."

"Not sure yet what the story is, Olive, but the building is surrounded by armed Gardai and there is some negotiating going on. I heard yer man, Larry, say something about 'two hours' on the phone. Not really sure and I don't feel like asking to be honest. My face is a result of asking a question."

A nervous silence settled within the library. Each of the group had concerns outside – a loved one waiting, a pet that depended on them, medication to be taken. None of them had any idea if they would survive or why this was happening to them.

***

Maxwell wasn't a wealthy man. He was comfortable financially, but isolation and loneliness stalked him daily. He had shed his past as a snake sheds its skin because of shame. He didn't like to dwell on it, but it bubbled to the surface now; he had let himself down badly in the course of his duties as bank manager. It was only one occasion, but the repercussions had not only affected his professional career but also his personal life.

Strangely enough, it was also a hostage situation some years ago in his branch in Dublin when members of his staff were also held at gunpoint. He was on his way out the back entrance for an appointment and, despite hearing screams, shouts and banging from the front office, he kept going, fast. He abandoned his duty as captain of his ship as, heart pounding, he scrambled to his life-saving Mercedes in the underground carpark.

As it turned out, just as the exit barrier of the carpark was raised and Maxwell zipped on to the narrow road at the back of the bank building, his assistant manager, with his hands in the air, had his foot pressed on an alarm behind the counter. The Gardai were alerted. The heist was aborted and there were no physical injuries. Maxwell, who made it home in jig time, feigned ignorance of the harrowing incident when he was notified by his assistant. He rushed back to the bank to support his staff.

The following day his life changed.

"I saw you running, you know." A young whipper snapper junior clerk accused him in front of his staff.

"What do you mean by that? The cheek of you to make such an accusation! I left the office for an appointment at 2.15, as my PA will confirm. I'm just sorry I wasn't on the premises at the time to take charge of the situation but well done to you all. You did very well in my absence."

It didn't wash. The staff looked askance as the young man hung him out to dry. He reported what he saw to the staff in great detail and to the investigating Gardai. Maxwell had to eventually admit that, while he was just about to turn the handle in the back door, he did hear threatening sounds and a lot of screaming and banging. He said he made a split-second decision to vacate the premises which, of course, he now regretted. CCTV verified his account.

Ultimately, he lost the confidence of his staff, some of whom were severely traumatised. He was offered a transfer to a small 'nothing' branch in a country town 'to ease staff relations'. His wife also left him in disgust, but they hadn't been hitting it off for quite a while anyway. His adult children were tolerant but cool towards him. Maxwell was a lonely man. He had never confided in anyone about his cowardice, but it clung to him like a bad smell.

He operated on a bravado type of superiority to cover up his insecurities and avoided getting close to people in case they found him out. It wasn't until Daniel joined the writing group that he feared he might be exposed. Firstly, Daniel looked remarkably like the young whelp that stitched him up and, secondly, he had that same attitude of fearlessness. Maxwell also knew that he was nosey. All of these things and fear of his past becoming known made Maxwell hate Daniel from the word go. Plus, he didn't like that fantasy sci fi stuff he wrote. Maxwell wondered if Daniel had escaped and if he might be the one to save the lot of them. He wasn't sure how he'd feel about that.

Chapter 10

Siobhan rubbed her shoulder. My good jacket Siobhan thought. She loved style and took time choosing her outfit daily. No matter the occasion she turned herself out well. Always matching her bag and shoes to a colour in her outfit. Remembering what her stylist used to say, no more than three colours should be worn at a time. Her clothes made her feel good and confident. How dare he poke me; she thought as she glared at JJ.

Siobhan had grown up with an abusive father and later married a man who turned out to be an abuser too. Although now at sixty-two and after a lot of counselling the memories and feelings from her childhood along with her failed marriage to Paddy were still vivid. Her mother, bless her, endured a lot to protect Siobhan while she was growing up.

Continually helping and encouraging Siobhan to study hard for college. Siobhan did not know that her grandfather had been abusive to her grandmother and mother. When Siobhan's father came on the scene, her mother felt marriage would be her way out of the abusive family home. It was, at least for a few years. Then he lost his job and turned to the bottle. In just a few months, he had turned into her grandfather, and began abusing her mother.

When Siobhan married Paddy, he was a kind, hardworking man. He was attentive to Siobhan and although they never had children, they both seemed content with each other. Unfortunately, history repeated itself. Paddy had a fall at work, hurting his back which forced him to stop working.

At first, he took the pain pills as prescribed by his doctor. As time passed, he took more, then he introduced the odd shot of alcohol. He felt the pills were more effective washed down with a shot of his favourite tipple. It didn't take long for Paddy to become dependent on both.

In a matter of months after Paddy's fall, his behaviour towards Siobhan changed. He began verbally abusing her. Even accusing her of having affairs. One evening he returned home from the pub, demanding his dinner, when Siobhan didn't retrieve the plate from the oven quick enough, he lashed out and slapped her face with his open hand. This was the first time he hit her. Attributing his behaviour to the loss of his job. She forgave him. That night, Siobhan lay in bed quietly sobbing, remembering the first time she saw her father hit her mother.

Fearing the worst was yet to come. She attempted to appease him and didn't confide in anyone. Siobhan put up with Paddy's behaviour in silence, until an unannounced visit from her mother. She couldn't hide her black eye. Her mother held her as they both cried. Leading her bruised sobbing daughter to the couch, she held her hand, spoke gently and reassuringly.

"We haven't spoken of your father in years my dear, I do think we need to talk. I know you don't blame me for his death, but I feel some blame lies with me. After years of taking his abuse, he began verbally abusing you, I was afraid he would start hitting you like he did me. Believe me Siobhan, I saw it coming. I was planning to leave him and take you with me. The night he died, he came home drunk, gave me another beating, this one was bad. He broke my arm and punched my face. I was afraid he was going to kill me. I tried to get to your bedroom to take you with me.

He caught me on the landing, drew back his fist to hit me again...I was so scared. I thought he was going to kill me, kill you. I pushed him hard on his chest...just to get away from him mind. But he stumbled backwards. He fell, tumbled down the stairs. I couldn't move. I just stood there, watching...in total shock if I'm honest. I froze on the spot, all the while quietly praying, he wouldn't get up. I waited for what seemed like forever, before I called for an ambulance. By the time the emergency services arrived it was too late. He was gone."

"Mam, why didn't you tell me?"

"I wanted to protect you. I still do. Look at you. It's history repeating itself. Get away from him, Siobhan. He will not change. You deserve so much better."

The next day Siobhan left Paddy and began divorce proceedings. That was twenty years ago, and she had been happy living alone ever since.

Chapter 11

The curtains of No. 6 Claremount Drive's front bedroom twitched, a set of hazel eyes peering out through a barely perceptible crack. The unmarked squad car was still there, parked several doors down. The Carpenter shook his head with mild amusement. The silver Hyundai i40, with two figures in the front seats, stood out like a sore thumb.

"Might as well turn on the blues," he muttered and turned away.

He returned to the bedroom window every few minutes for the next hour or two, making sure they were still there. At first, the constant surveillance had been wearisome, and he couldn't go to the local store without checking over his shoulder. But after a few weeks he'd started to enjoy the game of cat and mouse and the thought of how much it was costing the guards to watch him 24/7. According to one of his touts inside the force, it was blowing a massive hole in Dublin's budget.

The Carpenter grinned as he thought of the panic he'd sparked the previous month, when six men – all the same build and wearing the same clothes – left his house and quickly scattered in all directions. The rubber from the squad car's tyres was still imprinted on the road outside his front gate.

The smile died on his lips as his eyes strayed to the photo collage hanging above the king size bed. A memento of happier times. Although the house had become de facto headquarters of his organisation, it still couldn't fill the void Jan had left.

It was nearly six months to the day when he'd come back to find she'd packed her bags and taken the kid. All she'd left was a letter on the island unit to say she wouldn't be back. While it stung, it wasn't surprising – he'd come to expect it at some point, he realised. Jan liked to look respectable, volunteered for school events, went to Mass on Sunday mornings, kept the front garden picture perfect for the benefit of their neighbours. She managed to turn a blind eye to his work, ignored the steady flow of people who came and went through their back door, even overlooked his affairs. But what she couldn't get past, she had written in the letter, was being arrested outside the school with their son in the back seat and the other parents looking on in shock. Being handcuffed, shoved into the back of a squad car and taken to the local station was nothing new for The Carpenter – these days it happened nearly once or twice a month – but for Jan it was a humiliating experience. *Never again*, she vowed in ink.

The Carpenter shook his head, physically dispelling weak thoughts he knew would leave him sinking into a mental mire, and he forced himself to go through the plan once more. It was four months in the making, the result of many late nights with his lieutenants gathered around the kitchen table, arguing over who would do what, who to trust, who to pressure, what might go wrong or whether they were mad to even go through with it.

Some of them had misgivings, he knew, but The Carpenter was determined to pull it off. This would be his magnum opus, a daring daylight raid planned and executed to perfection, a haul big enough for him to retire to a small island somewhere in the Caribbean. A private paradise far from prying eyes and the long arm of the law. A peace he'd earned after years of hard graft, clawing his way through the mud to rise to the top.

The smile returned as he thought of white sandy beaches, crystal clear water, warmth in the sun, a drink in one hand and a young woman on his arm. In his line of work, retirement was a rarity – most of the gang lords he'd met on the way up were either dead or in prison. The Carpenter was determined to avoid either route. In quieter moments, he browsed through the real estate websites in search of his new home and had already narrowed down a few options in the seven-figure range. *Almost in reach*, he thought.

His phone pinged and he read the short message with satisfaction. The cogs had begun to move and, so far, everything was going to plan. Five minutes later, he was in his front garden, making a show of weeding the flowerbed but keeping a close eye on his watch. He made sure his official stalkers had a good view of him – they would be his alibi when shit hit the fan thirty miles down the road.

Chapter 12

Sadie knew she had to get JJ on his own.

"Hey, I need the loo really bad," she announced loudly, looking towards Larry.

"Me too." Siobhan and Betty said in unison.

"Shut up and stay where you are." Larry's responded as he pointed the gun in Sadie's direction.

"Please…" She pleaded. She nodded towards JJ. "He can stand guard at the door. We can't escape. You've already made sure all doors and windows are locked. Come on, have a heart, we could be here for a while yet."

Larry wasn't in the mood for female persuasion regardless of how vulnerable Sadie looked. However, on reflection he had no idea if the detective inspector would adhere to his demand and arrange safe passage out of the library in the two-hour timeframe he had given.

"Go on then, one at a time," he barked, giving JJ the nod to go with Sadie and warning that they'd pay if there was any 'funny business'.

JJ bustled about, tearing the duct tape off Sadie's wrists. She winced but kept close to JJ as they approached to door leading to the corridor. This was her chance to be alone with him for the short walk to and from the toilets. She hoped that reminding him of his past connection to her brother would make him see sense. He might rethink his loyalty to Larry and help them escape.

As they turned into the corridor, Sadie spoke in a whisper.

"Hey John Joe, do you remember Matthew Conlon from school and the boxing club?"

"How the hell do you know I went to school with Mattie Conlon?" he asked.

"He's my younger brother. I remember you two were in the boxing club together. Our dads used to say you were the one most likely to make it professionally. Do you remember?"

"Yea, I was better than Mattie, and he was good, but he dropped out after the first year. I loved boxing."

"Think what Mattie would say if he knew you were being cruel to his sister and my friends," she said in a low voice.

JJ reacted angrily.

"To hell with you and Mattie, I've moved on from those days," he snarled, pushing Sadie towards the toilet door. "Get your skates on or Larry will come looking for us."

Sadie persisted hoping there was a vestige of the young lad she remembered still there.

"Please, John Joe, think about what you're doing. You were never a bad kid. What would your parents think of you now terrorising innocent people? You can stop this nonsense and get Larry to let us go."

JJ had heard enough. He pushed Sadie through the bathroom door and pulled it closed. While he waited for her for come out, his thoughts drifted back to his childhood, to simpler, uncomplicated days with his decent parents trying to do their best for him. He thought of his father up at the crack of dawn five days a week, collecting papers from the local newspaper depot and delivering them to shops around the county. Hell or high water, his father would be at home waiting for the kids to come in from school in the afternoons, asking how they got on, kicking a ball around with them on the green until dinner time.

He had a lump in his throat thinking about his father's pride in his boxing and how his face would light up telling his mother how great he was. His mother would laugh and say, 'Sure isn't he a chip off the old block,' as she tousled his hair playfully.

He didn't wonder where it all went wrong; he knew too well. He had made some very bad decisions. Getting in with a bad crowd was the first, experimenting with a hit of cocaine the second and it was downhill from there on. His boxing career had slipped through his fingers as the drugs messed with his brain until he lost everything, even the ability to think for himself. He was hooked and needed to follow anyone who could provide him with drugs or the means to get them.

He straightened his shoulders and resumed his air of bravado as he heard the lock being turned in the loo door. Sadie emerged, hoping her words had sparked something in JJ's head that would trigger his better nature.

"You can still do the right thing, John Joe," she said quietly.

"It's too late for that, I'm involved now, and I can't back out. Besides, they made me a promise. This is a one-off job and I'll never have to worry about money again. Plus, he has the gun."

Just then, Larry stuck his head around the corner.

"What in blue blazes is keeping you two? Get to hell back here fast."

"Right boss!" JJ responded as he roughly shoved Sadie back to the group. He quickly secured her hands with duct tape and beckoned her to take her place on the floor. He turned to Siobhan and dragged her to her feet, removed the duct tape and pushed her towards the corridor. The next fifteen minutes or so were taken up by JJ escorting the group one at a time to the bathroom.

Chapter 13

Olive was the only member of the group who didn't pay a visit to the toilet. Her mind was filled with thoughts of her husband. She wondered if he was enjoying the golf with his friends and what he would make of her predicament.

Pascal had taken up golf the year before he retired from lecturing in the history department of University College Dublin. He loved the sport and had made a few good friends. Since retiring he played most days. It had been Pascal's turn to arrange an away golfing trip. He decided it would be in Cork over three days. Olive hugged her husband goodbye that morning after breakfast. Pascal had promised to call her after dinner that evening.

With a wave, Pascal drove out of the driveway to pick up his three golfing buddies. Olive felt sad now and very much alone thinking of the hug she shared with Pascal that morning, making her miss him even more.

Olive had never experienced anything like this. Realising these thugs meant business, she was at a loss as to how things would play out. She reckoned the joker with the gun was not sure of his plan to escape as he paced the floor, glancing frequently at the clock on the wall.

When the group were secured with duct tape again, Olive ended up sitting next to Siobhan, observing Larry pacing away from the group towards the children's section. JJ sat on the edge of a table at the other end of the room. Olive needed to know what happened before she was forced to come out of hiding.

"What's the latest?" she whispered, hoping Siobhan would fill her in. Siobhan held her head close to Olive while aware of any movement from the two captors.

"He's given the detective two hours to come up with a plan for safe passage out of here for himself and the other idiot over there," she whispered.

"How long ago was that?"

"I think thirty or forty minutes ago," Siobhan whispered.

"Forty minutes exactly," Betty said, surprising the others. She appeared to be deep in thought, staring at Larry with an intensity that was quite unsettling.

"There's something very familiar about him, his facial expression, his gestures, like I know him from somewhere, yet I know I don't."

Chapter 14

Daniel grunted, his face reddening with effort as he tried to force open the only window in the meeting room that had a handle. His arm muscles quivered, and he gasped and let go, cursing the unyielding brass handle.

As he caught his breath, his eyes scanned the room for something he could use to pry open the window. The other members of the writing group had left their bags scattered across the table and the floor. Siobhan's handbag was full of old receipts and chocolate wrappers, but nothing useful. Maxwell had left his vintage leather briefcase against the leg of the chair. Inside was the latest draft of his book, as well as a handwritten diary, bound in black leather. Daniel's hand hovered over the latter. He'd taken an instant dislike to Maxwell the first time they'd met around this table. The older man seemed to think he automatically deserved Daniel's respect simply because he was almost twice his age, and his writing was more highbrow than Daniel's. He opened the first page, an entry dating to more than a year ago. Daniel flicked through the pages, searching for a more recent date, then found what he was looking for. Maxwell had written a short entry the day they'd met at the library, mostly about how the group's newest member was thoroughly unlikable and, on the face of it, a writer without talent.

"What an absolute wanker," Daniel muttered, his cheeks turning a fiery red. "He thinks he knows me so well. Let's see what secrets you're hiding from the rest of us, eh?"

He slipped the diary into his back pocket and turned his attention to Sadie's small, trendy rucksack, which had been hidden under the table out of sight. Tucked inside a small purse, he found a miniature, red-handled penknife set on a keyring. He crossed to the window and tried to jimmy it open using each of the tools, but nothing worked. He shoved it in his pocket with the diary.

Frustrated, Daniel spent several more fruitless minutes trying to open the window by hand, silently wondering why he spent several evenings a week working out in the gym if he couldn't open a blasted window. For a moment, he contemplated trying to smash the frosted glass but decided against it, realising the resultant crash would draw the men down on him like a tonne of bricks. He took a deep breath, grasped the handle with both hands, then yanked as hard as he could. With a crack, the handle came loose, and he stumbled backwards, falling over a chair.

"What was that? Did you hear that?" he heard a voice, muffled by distance, say in the library. "JJ, go check it out. Take the gun."

Daniel froze, caught between fight and flight. For a few milliseconds he considered standing his ground, tackling whoever was heading this way. Maybe he could save the day. Instead, he scooped up the broken window handle and bolted for the corner where a bookcase stood and wedged himself behind it, holding his breath. Seconds later, the door burst open, and someone strode inside. Daniel could hear his heart thumping, a sound that seemed to fill the room. Seconds ticked by like hours.

"Is someone in here?" a male's voice barked. "If you don't show your face now, it'll only be worse for you when I find you."

The man barged through the room, knocking the table over, throwing chairs, even yanking open the bookcase Daniel was hiding behind. A silence fell and Daniel could almost feel the man's eyes scanning the room. His lungs silently pleaded for air, pain spreading through his chest. And then the door to the room was slammed shut again and Daniel released the breath he'd been holding, relief washing over him.

"There's nobody there." He heard the voice call out, fading as it moved away. "Maybe the wind or something. All the windows and doors are still locked."

Daniel shoved his way out from behind the bookcase and waited for a moment, ears straining to make sure the man had gone back into the library. He was suddenly embarrassed by how he'd reacted, running and hiding. He'd always thought he'd fight if he ever found himself in a situation like that. Daniel often had trouble sleeping and he'd lie in bed for ages, his mind's eye playing out scenarios in which he was always the hero. Foiling a robbery at the post office and saving the pretty worker, Michelle, who was always deeply, deeply grateful; sprinting across the main street in Newbridge to save a small child frozen in the path of an oncoming lorry; leading the resistance to the sudden onslaught of a zombie herd and saving the town from being completely over-run. But he'd had a chance to take charge, be a hero in real life and he'd fallen at the first hurdle.

He swallowed and, with an effort, pushed those feelings to the back of his mind and considered his next move. He checked his phone but there was still no signal, and he couldn't pick up the library wi-fi in this room. He turned on his phone's data connection and tried to make a call on WhatsApp, but it wouldn't work. He checked the Vodafone app and quickly realised he'd forgotten to top up the day before.

"Every bloody time," he muttered as he shoved the phone back in his pocket.

Daniel crept to the far corner of the room where two doors adjoined and considered his options. They were limited. The door to his left opened onto a corridor running parallel to the back of the building – storerooms and toilets and offices on the left, the main library on the right. One possibility could be to get down the full length of the corridor without making a sound and more importantly, not being spotted. He could then try to access the lobby through a door and get outside. He thought about darting from one room to the next but decided he couldn't risk getting caught in a smaller space with nowhere to hide.

He turned his attention to the door to his right. It led to a smaller part of the library, and not too far away was another exit onto the Athgarvan Road. A stumbling block was the amount of open space to cross, and he reckoned the chances of getting through without being rumbled were slim to none. And he definitely couldn't get out through the meeting room window now the handle had snapped.

His eyes drifted to the ceiling. He knew that above the ceiling tiles there was a narrow crawlspace running the length of the building. There'd been a talk on the history of the library last year when one of the speakers had mentioned it off-hand, and he'd always wanted to see what was up there. If he could get into the crawlspace, he could move from rafter to rafter and get out through the ceiling in the foyer, though he'd have to be careful with his footing. One wrong move and he'd come crashing down into the room below.

Daniel gently pulled the table back on its legs, quietly lifted a chair onto its surface and awkwardly clambered up. He reached out and pushed one of the ceiling tiles out of its frame to reveal a narrow space shrouded in darkness. A steel girder ran across the room, and he grabbed the edge, grunting as he hauled himself up, ducking to avoid a pipe overhead. Once he settled himself, he pulled out his phone, the torch lighting the way ahead. He could see a long line of wooden rafters disappearing into the gloom, surrounded by pipes and wiring. He replaced the ceiling tile, paused, got his bearings and crawled onto the first rafter, staying low. There was a slight creak and dust slowly wafted into the air, but the rafter held. He gave a low sigh of relief and reached out for the second one.

Outside, the day was warm with a pleasant breeze, but inside the crawlspace the heat was stifling. After just a few minutes, Daniel's wavy black hair was wet with sweat and rivulets ran down his cheeks and neck, disappearing below the collar of his shirt. His head was beginning to pound. Memories floated back of a family holiday in the south of France when he was a child. They'd taken a trip to Carcassonne, a great fortified city that dominated the surrounding landscape. After more than two hours of wandering through the streets in the sweltering heat, he and his parents had taken refuge in the cathedral which had felt like a wonderful icebox. They'd spent the next hour or so inside and Daniel wished he was in that cool cathedral right that moment instead of crawling through the library ceiling.

He wondered what was happening to the others. He could hear two men muttering not far away, an edge to their voices. He recognised the young voice of Sadie but couldn't decipher what she was saying. He could hear Maxwell's name being mentioned although he couldn't hear the old man himself talking. He gave a small smile at the thought of Maxwell trussed up and gagged. It was as if the universe had heard and judged him. As soon as that thought entered his head, his phone torch quenched, and he was plunged into suffocating darkness. Daniel suppressed a curse as his fingers scrabbled at the phone, clicking at buttons, but there was nothing. The phone was dead, and he still had over half the distance to go. He took a deep breath and reached out, grasping for the next rafter which was a little further than he thought.

As he blindly crawled forward, particles of dust that had lain undisturbed for years floated through the air and he felt an increasing urge to sneeze. Daniel stopped at the edge of a rafter and grasped his nose, suppressing the sneeze with every fibre of his being. After several moments of agony, the urge passed, and he relaxed as he crawled forward again.

Suddenly, as he reached forward, he realised he was in trouble. His stomach lurched as he fell forward into thin air, gasping as his forehead cracked against the edge of the next rafter. Stars burst behind his eyes and for a moment he was in agony. He steeled himself not to cry out in pain. He blindly grasped for something to steady himself on and he stayed where he was for minutes that felt like hours, trying to regain his composure.

As he lay there, the pain subsiding, he heard a woman's voice talking somewhere just below him. It took a moment for him to recognise it was Betty, the librarian on duty that evening. He realised he'd strayed a little off course and was somewhere over the reception area. Still, all he had to do was keep moving forward and he'd be over the lobby, down through the ceiling and out to freedom. His spirits brightened at the thought of being able to get help and save the day. It also struck him that he knew one of the reporters in the local newspaper. Perhaps they could come down and take a photo. He wasn't entirely sure what was going on but, whatever it was, it would surely be front page news.

Before he set off again, Daniel took another deep breath, inhaling a lungful of dust particles. Another sneeze built and he grabbed his nose just before it thundered out of him.

"Whew," he muttered. "That was a close one."

He moved forward and cracked his knee against the nearest rafter with a loud thunk. Daniel froze, tears welling in his eyes from the pain, and he prayed neither of the men in the library had heard it.

Chapter 15

Detective Chief Inspector Ciaran Darcy was hopping mad. Sergeant Tom Moore knew that this hostage situation in the library was interfering with the DCI's plans or put another way, his wife's plans. Darcy was a force to be reckoned with in the station but at home he didn't wear the trousers.

"She who must be obeyed has given me instructions to be home by five o'clock latest this evening." He had told Sergeant Moore earlier in day. "It's our 30th wedding anniversary and there's a big 'do' organised for this evening. It's more than my life's worth to be late."

Darcy had already let it slip about the party earlier in the month when they were getting the roster together, telling him about his daughter coming home for Australia specifically to organise the event.

"Yourself and Bernadette are invited, of course," he told Moore. He was clearly delighted in his own gruff way about all the fuss. More than anything, he was thrilled to see his daughter again home from Australia.

It was around lunchtime and Darcy's desk had been cleared by three, fifteen minutes before all hell broke loose. Some petty criminals had decided that Derby Day in the Curragh would be a good day to rob one of the local bookies. Their get-away plan, if they had one, had gone belly up and they were now terrifying the life out of a harmless group of people in the library. They were holding them as hostages at gunpoint.

Darcy was now standing legs apart in his smart blue inspector's uniform surrounded by a sea of Gardai on the bridge facing the library. A heavily armed unit were standing on alert along with the usual unarmed Gardai.

That face would sour milk, thought Moore, as he saw Darcy bark orders to surround the building and find out who was in there, their names, addresses, etc. He wanted the phone number of the library to make contact and to assess the situation internally. In his right hand he had a megaphone.

"No lives must be lost," he ordered his men. "Negotiation is the key here so keep alert and report anything you observe back to me immediately. Go cautiously."

He had instructed Sergeant Moore to block all access points around the town and to divert traffic. This was a tall order on Derby Day when the town was jammers; it was a bloody nightmare. The usual whirring of helicopters bringing the great and good of horse racing to the Curragh had receded to clear space for a Garda helicopter. *There'll be hell to play when the big shots are discommoded,* thought Moore.

Moore decided to give Darcy a wide berth for the moment, after ensuring that roads leading into the town were blocked and manned and diversion signs erected.

"There's a snowball's chance in hell that Darcy will be celebrating his anniversary this evening," Moore said to his next in line, Jack Fitzgerald. "The poor bugger's in for it when he gets home."

"Bad timing all right. That was a powerful write-up he got in The Garda Review last month. In fairness to him, he's one of the good ones. You'd always feel he'd do the right thing and uphold the law with a fair hand. He's strict, and I wouldn't like to cross him, but there's a bit of softness about him too. I think he'd support you if you needed it."

"Ah, you're right, you're right, Jack." agreed Moore. "He's not the worst. I feel sorry for him that he got caught up in this today of all days. C'mon, let's head over to him and see what's what."

Chapter 16

Miriam Darcy was waved off by her daughter, Georgina, with instructions not to be home until the afternoon.

"I have everything under control, and I won't leave the house until everything is delivered and in place for tonight," she told her mum. "It's your day for lots of pampering. Go off and enjoy yourself. You deserve it."

Her three children, at Georgina's prompting, had organised an appointment at Miriam's favourite beauty salon for eleven am followed by a hair appointment at one pm. This would give her ample time to get home and get herself ready for the party. The back garden looked exquisite with roses blooming, summer bedding bursting with colour and trees providing shade from the hot summer sun. Lights and lanterns hung from branches of the trees. Strips of lights around the perimeter of the garden would create a wonderful festive atmosphere later in the evening as it got darker. White tablecloths covered the trestle tables which would be graced with flowers and night lights. It had taken a lot of planning and Miriam was amazed at how Georgina organised most of the evening from Australia. Once she got over jet lag, she zoomed into action again. It seemed effortless and took a lot of worry from Miriam's shoulders.

Luxuriating in the softly dimmed treatment room, warm towels wrapped around her, Miriam sighed as her favourite beautician, Sarah, massaged lightly scented oil on her face and shoulders. Her firm hands glided from her neck, caressed her shoulders and unknotted any tension spots at the back of her neck. Miriam could feel herself relaxing and her skin soak up the goodness of the oil.

"And your daughter, Georgina, has come all the way from Australia to celebrate with you. Isn't that wonderful? Is it long since you've seen her?" asked Sarah.

"We went to see her in Sydney last year but it's so good to have her home. Tracey and Pete haven't stopped chatting and laughing since she arrived on Tuesday. The fact that she works in event management is a real bonus for the party. She has taken charge of everything."

"Marvellous. Well, you just relax there for ten minutes and I'll be back to continue your treatment. We need to let the goodness of the oil seep into your skin." She placed a soft warm cloth on Miriam's face and silently left the room.

Where did all those years go to, wondered Miriam as she lay there. She let her mind drift back to when she met Ciaran thirty-three years ago at a night club in Cork. He was a young recruit, six months out of Templemore Training College and she was attracted to him straight away. Turned out, he felt the same. Over thirty years later their love for each other had deepened and matured and they felt lucky to be happy together when so many couples they knew had drifted apart. They could still laugh and be happy in each other's company.

Ciaran was ambitious and Miriam supported him all the way, encouraging him to do the sergeant's exam. They had moved house several times when Ciaran's work required it. It wasn't always easy with young children, but their most recent posting six years ago when Ciaran was appointed Detective Chief Inspector was the best ever. Miriam loved her spacious house on the outskirts of Dublin.

There had been worrying times, particularly when Ciaran was in the Special Branch when the kids were small, but thankfully he had stayed safe. But you never knew from one day to the next. As she lay there, she said a silent prayer, thanking God for keeping Ciaran and the kids safe and for giving them such a good life. Feeling thoroughly relaxed after her treatment, she felt a coffee was in order before her hair appointment. As she sipped her coffee, she decided to call Ciaran and remind him, yet again, to come home early.

"Don't you worry, love. Everything is quiet here and I'm just going to tie up a few loose ends and clear my desk. I'll be home in plenty of time. We've lots to celebrate after thirty years, haven't we? You're still the love of my life you know," he told Miriam - after checking that the door to his office was closed. He was a loving but private man, not given to public displays of affection.

"It's worth a celebration, 30 years of married bliss," Miriam told him. "We've been lucky. See you later so." She ended the call.

Chapter 17

Siobhan thought quickly as she walked through the door and into the corridor that ran behind the library's reception, trying to figure out what to do. She knew instinctively that it was Daniel who made the noise and that he was somewhere in the roof, and she didn't want to see him fall into the hands of their captors too. But what could she do to prevent that?

She wondered what Daniel was doing up there. She recalled him saying he was going to get out through the window of the meeting room and go get help, but obviously that hadn't happened. Something must have gone wrong, and he'd got into the roof instead. Siobhan didn't know Daniel all that well, though she did know he was quite sure of himself and always ready to jump into action. She just hoped he wasn't about to do something rash.

The noise had sounded like it had come from the roof over the reception area and the corridor, and she presumed he was heading across the building in a bid to escape. She wondered if he knew the crawlspace above their heads had been bricked off before the lobby area and hoped he was heading in a different direction. Siobhan knew she needed to distract JJ a little longer and give Daniel a chance to make it outside. JJ was hot on her heels and, when she hesitated even for a moment outside the small office, he shoved her forward.

"Go on," he snarled. "I know there has to be a way into the roof somewhere around here. Where is it?"

"If there is, I don't know of it," she replied, trying to keep her voice calm. "That sound was probably an animal trapped up there in the roof. A bird, possibly. Look, I'm sure you both have enough on your plate at the moment without crawling around inside the roof after a stuck crow or whatever it is."

JJ shook his head and gave her another shove, and she flung out an arm to stop herself colliding with the wall. Siobhan did her best not to react in anger, knowing that keeping her head and her wits about her was the best chance of getting through this ordeal. It still didn't seem quite real. Being caught up in the middle of a hostage situation was something you read about in books or see in movies, not something you expect to experience first-hand in real-life, and certainly not in a town like Newbridge. She wondered what had brought the two men to their door. Clearly, they were on the run from the Gardaí, but why? What had they done? Perhaps they had tried to rob the bank nearby, although she didn't think banks carried that much cash these days to make a robbery worthwhile.

Siobhan knew that whatever the men had done, if the Gardaí were after them and they were willing to take a group of innocent people hostage, they were dangerous, and the writing group needed to stay calm and avoid sending them over the edge. Her mind briefly flitted back to her childhood in Kildare town. She knew all about dangerous men and what they were capable of.

"Do you really need to treat us like that?" she said coolly. "We haven't done anything to either of you to deserve it."

JJ glared at her.

"You lot were lying about there not being anyone else missing," he grunted. "And then that woman mysteriously appeared from nowhere. You're lying now too, I know it."

She shook her head. "Like I said, I've never heard of an entrance into the roof, and as best I know there's no attic up there. All I can do is search through the rooms with you."

She opened the door to the office, looked back at JJ and raised her eyebrow.

Chapter 18

The noise of his knee striking the rafter had been amplified inside the crawlspace and it filled Daniel's eardrums. He didn't move for more than a minute, heart racing, fear coursing through his veins. The men below would certainly have heard that sound. He heard one of them shout and his entire body tensed.

"Ye're a pack of lying scumbags," a man's voice roared out. "You'd better find whoever is hiding."

Daniel could feel his heart thudding against his chest. He forced himself to move, reaching for the closest rafter, pulling his knees onto it, ignoring the pain from his kneecaps, then stretching his arm out to grasp the next one. He moved slowly, making sure of his footing before moving on, acutely aware of all the dust he was breathing and ready to stop the next sneeze from giving him away.

From somewhere behind him, Daniel heard a scraping noise. He turned his neck, trying to see whatever it was and hoping, for the first and only time in his life, that a rat was waiting to pounce. Instead, he saw a chink of light as one of the ceiling tiles below the rafters was lifted out of place. Seconds later, a head popped through, followed by an arm and a torch, its light illuminating the dark space.

Daniel kept crawling, veering sideways into the shadows of one of the wooden A frames holding the roof up, hoping that whoever was back there hadn't spotted him. He almost had a heart attack when a voice called out.

"Who's up there?" a man's voice asked. "We heard you making noise, we know you're hiding up here. You better come out now before we have to go up and get you, otherwise you'll be sorry, I promise you that. Don't make this any harder than it needs to be."

Part of Daniel wanted to crawl out, put his hands up and get it over with, but he sat there, hidden from sight by the A frame and praying that the man didn't actually know he was there and was just chancing his arm. The way forward was still cloaked in darkness, but he knew he couldn't be far from the lobby now. He could hear different voices coming from somewhere outside the library, people barking orders, and he wondered if the guards had been alerted to what was happening.

"Alright," the man called out. "I'm coming up to get you so. You'll be sorry you didn't just come out and show yourself, that's for sure."

Daniel risked a quick glance around the frame. His heart skipped a beat as he realised the man wasn't bluffing – the torch was resting on one of the rafters and a dark figure was climbing up into the crawlspace. Daniel started moving again, doing his utmost not to make any noise. He reached out for another rafter but instead there was empty space and, before he could stop himself, he was falling headfirst, crashing through the ceiling tiles and into the room below. He lay on the floor, gasping for breath, his head thumping. He tried to get up and, as he did, pain shot through his right leg and he cried out, falling back to the ground.

A man stepped forward into his field of vision, and, as Daniel's vision cleared, his blood ran cold.

There was an icy chill behind the man's eyes, an unforgiving stare that promised nothing good.

"Well, would you look at this!" the man said slowly, each word dripping with menace. "What have we here then?"

Chapter 19

Well, well, well, Sergeant Tom Moore thought, *a colossal fuckup. Who would have thought it?* He swivelled around taking in the massive police presence at the northern end of Newbridge on Derby Day when usually all Garda resources would have been trained on the Curragh Racecourse.

Around him flashing lights from every Garda car in the county whirled shouting their presence. The bridge was a sea of blue and white, a line of vehicles blocking all ways in and out of the town. There must have been fifty rank and file standing around in groups chatting in the late afternoon sun. Sergeant Moore felt the heat through his formal blues. The belt of his trousers was let out to the last notch in a vain attempt to pull his rotund belly into shape. Taking off his cap, he wiped the sweat from his shiny scalp with a paper hankie, before replacing the cap in the correct position. There were those in his profession who didn't put much store by their appearance. Sergeant Tom Moore wasn't one of them.

Overhead a helicopter hovered. It was only a matter of time before Newbridge would be splattered all over the news. He wondered what Bernadette would think when she saw the news this evening - probably relief that she wouldn't have to go to the Darcys' anniversary party. He knew when he married her what a frightful snob she was. His mother warned him about marrying 'above his station', as she put it. Tom hadn't seen it that way. Bernadette was smart and funny. The daughter of a leading solicitor, she trained to be an architect, then abandoned everything when their first daughter was born. Twenty-five years later she still calls herself an architect. She never mentions the fact that she hasn't practised her profession in all those years. Even Tom's mother agreed that Bernadette had exquisite taste. Their bungalow on the outskirts of the Curragh had featured in several glossy magazines.

They also owned a city centre apartment. They bought it for the girls. It was cheaper to buy one than pay rents for them during their college years. Now that it was empty Bernadette planned to renovate it for their own use. She planned a winter of plays and music events in Dublin. Her social calendar was already practically fully booked until next spring.

The staccato beat of the helicopter blades intruded into his thoughts. Staring upwards he realised he was right in their line of sight and that would not do. Better to stay in the background. Especially now.

"That's enough tittle tattle," Sergeant Moore roared at the nearest group, "this is a hostage situation, not a feckin' tea party."

Detective Chief Inspector Darcy beckoned him over.

"Check the cordon. It looks like the bridge is covered but I'm not sure about the Athgarvan Road. Make sure there is no escape route," DCI Darcy looked anxiously at his watch.

"The timing sucks," Tom Moore said, "Miriam is going to be pissed."

"I'm hoping it's going to be over fairly quickly, and I don't have to tell her," Ciaran Darcy said, "I mean, I don't think she'd believe me anyway. I mean, who takes hostages in a library? What the actual fuck?"

"You might not have to tell her," Tom Moore pointed at the helicopter circling overhead.

"Hopefully, it'll all be resolved by the six o'clock news."

Chapter 20

Marie glanced at her watch, wondering where her husband was. It had been over an hour now since she'd felt pain in her pregnant belly and her anxiety was growing by the minute. Where was he? Larry hadn't said where he was, but that wasn't unusual. He'd always been a secretive type and Marie sometimes wondered if she really knew Larry – the real Larry – at all.

Her hands subconsciously patted her belly and she hoped everything would be alright. After she'd miscarried, it was over a year before they even thought about trying again. Marie's thoughts flicked back to that horrible time in their lives and for a moment she allowed herself to dwell on the worst possible scenario before making a conscious effort to push those thoughts out of her mind. This time, everything would be fine. Her due date was two weeks away, so at worst it would be an early labour, she reassured herself.

The minutes ticked by and there was still so sign of Larry. She went to the bathroom for the fourth time that morning and, when she came out, strode to the front door, hoping to see his car parked in the drive and an apologetic look on his face as he rushed towards her. But the driveway was empty.

Marie took a deep breath and went into the kitchen, grabbed her phone and called him again. Like the last twenty times, the call went straight to voicemail, and she cursed him, wondering where on earth he could be. A small, niggling, intrusive and unwelcome thought in the back of her mind wondered if Larry was with his brother. Matt was a habitual drug user and it had got to the point where Larry had started ignoring his phone calls, knowing there would be some sort of plea for money at the other end of the line. But turning your back completely on family was no easy task. Larry had certainly been a little different for the past few weeks, somewhat distant and quieter, thought Marie, but she had assumed that he – like her – was simply worried about the pregnancy and what lay ahead.

Pain assaulted her stomach with a vengeance as the growing intensity of the contractions gripped her body, almost forcing her to her knees. She clutched at the table for support, groaning and fighting back tears as she punched Larry's number on her phone. Yet again, it went to voicemail.

"Larry, for heaven's sake, where are you?" she growled down the phone. "I'm after getting another pain here and I'm heading to the hospital right this instant. I think the baby's coming early. You better call me back as soon as you get this. I'm really worried now, and I need you here,"

She hung up the phone, grabbed the go bag by the stairs and edged her way painfully out the front door. "He better have a very good excuse for not being here," she muttered as she headed for her car.

Chapter 21

Olive analysed their situation. Beside her Maxwell was visibly shaking, his usual outward bluster deflated by his struggle to breathe through his damaged nose. The duct tape bit into her wrists every time she tried to make herself comfortable as if that were even possible in a situation like this. Olive straightened her back against the counter, trying to roll her shoulders to release some of the tension gathering there. Years of pilates had kept her body nimble but even as fit as she was, at her age, sitting on the floor with her wrists trussed up behind her was no easy feat. Olive shuddered to think how the others were coping.

She sneaked a sideways glance. They were all lined up, backs against the reception counter beside her. Maxwell, Sadie, the librarian while Larry stood in front of them looking from one worried expression to the next. They could hear JJ's voice from the corridor where he pushed Siobhan in front of him minutes earlier. The whole building was eerily quiet apart from Maxwell's laboured breathing.

Above their heads, the ceiling creaked, and they all looked up. Suddenly the ceiling collapsed in a hail of plaster and dust. They heard a man scream and a thud as he hit the ground. As the dust settled, Daniel lay groaning in the middle of the rubble.

"Well, well," Larry said, "What have we here then?"

"Bloody eejit." JJ's manic laughter sounded from the roof space as the building settled back into itself.

Larry looked up and yelled, "get down here."

On the ground, Daniel tried to sit up but squealed in pain and fell back. Larry grabbed him by the collar and tried to drag him towards the others.

"Stop," Sadie shouted, "he's hurt. Stop it."

"Shut it, now, or I'll shut you up for good," Larry waved the gun in Sadie's direction, "JJ, get in here."

JJ arrived back in the main room, pulling Siobhan roughly with him.

"Help me drag this fucker over to the rest of them."

Between them, they dragged Daniel, ignoring his cries of pain, and pushed him up against the reception counter beside Olive. The pain must have been intense, as Daniel lost consciousness and slid over onto Olive's lap.

"We need an ambulance," Olive looked straight at Larry with steel authority, "that was quite a fall. He may be seriously injured."

"Shut it, all of you," Larry roared.

Sadie spoke up. "At least let me look at him. I might be able to help him."

"I said shut up."

"It would be in your best interest to at least let her try." Olive spoke quietly but firmly. "First responders can make the difference between life and death."

They all mumbled their agreement, with even JJ glancing over at Larry, who nodded his assent. He had no choice really. Sadie, her first aid experience in demand again, should take a look at Daniel to assess his injuries. Just as well someone had some idea of what to do with the boy.

"Okay, okay, but you try anything..." Larry didn't need to finish his sentence. The gun in his hand was enough to silence his prisoners.

He pulled Sadie forward and signalled to JJ to cut through the duct tape binding her wrists. She rubbed them and wiggled her fingers to ease the stiffness and get the blood flowing through them again before she made her way over to Daniel and checking his pulse.

Sadie gave a brief smile to the others, and with her back to their captors, gave them a thumbs up. Daniel stirred and moaned. Sadie spoke to him gently and helped him lie on his side so she could get a better look at his right leg.

"I need scissors."

"Not a chance," JJ said.

"Well, you do it then. I need to see if there's anything broken."

Larry knelt beside her and cut Daniel's right trouser leg from hem to hip. Sadie examined his lower leg tenderly. She couldn't feel any obvious break. He didn't seem to have any head injuries but, Sadie told everyone, you just wouldn't know what internal injuries he had until he was checked over by a doctor. She confirmed that he was alive but luckily was unconscious as he would have a lot of pain and discomfort from falling from such a height.

With an unexpected air of authority Sadie addressed Larry. "OK. The story is that he needs medical assistance from a qualified medic straight away. I need Olive's help to make him more comfortable when, or should I say if, he regains consciousness. I would urge you to get medical help or he might die."

Looking straight into JJ's eyes, Sadie confronted him in no uncertain terms.

"Do you want to face charges of murder or manslaughter on top of hostage taking and whatever else you've done," she asked firmly.

"You're a cheeky bitch, aren't you? Get on with it. I'll let the cops know we need medical assistance and don't try any tricks or... I'll cut your hands off myself, you won't be so brave then, will you?" he barked.

Larry muttered expletives under his breath as he turned away from the group. JJ went over and whispered in his ear. Larry swatted him away like he was an annoying insect. He walked away, around the corner out of sight with JJ behind him. They could hear the door into the staff corridor closing behind them, and the sound of raised voices. He was clearly furious at JJ for causing the crash landing and could be heard giving him a good dressing down in the corridor.

Olive leaned forward and whispered to Sadie, 'the keys. Top drawer reception desk.'

Sadie understood immediately and didn't waste a second. She disappeared from their view and reappeared thirty seconds later with a set of keys, too bulky to hide under her tight skirt and top. She waved them at Betty, "Yes, that's them."

They all froze as the sound of the staff door opening carried into the room.

"Here," Olive nodded at the pocket in her layered tunic top, "inside pocket."

Sadie placed the keys into Olive's inner pocket and quickly went back to her position beside Daniel, who was now fully conscious and groaning.

The phone rang, and for a millisecond, everyone stopped breathing. Olive felt like she was in a freeze-frame, as if she had stopped the action in the middle of a drama series to get a cup of tea. Then Larry moved, and the illusion shattered. He moved behind them to the reception desk and picked up the phone.

"Don't know what you heard, but nothing going on in here. We're waiting for our safe passage. One hour and twenty minutes."

JJ laughed and jiggled around like he was in training for a boxing match. He pointed the gun at Sadie and laughed again as they all recoiled in horror. Slowly he pointed the gun at each of them in turn. Olive closed her eyes, wishing this ordeal were over, cursing herself for not going on the golf trip with Pascal. Why hadn't she learned to play golf years ago? She could be at dinner now in the clubhouse with the other wives, talking about birdies and double bogeys, instead of sitting here trussed up like a chicken on the floor of the library.

Pascal will be ringing her later, and she wondered if she would be home in time to take his call. After his round of golf, there would be dinner and drinks, and it could be late before he got around to calling her. Her belongings were still in the back room with everyone else's, the mobile on silent as it always was during the writer's group meetings. Not that she expected a call from anyone else. There was no one else to miss her. Not since Jenny died. Her grief swiped her sideways again. It was always there, bubbling under the surface, ready to erupt at the strangest times. It had been over two years now, and every time she thought she was coming to terms with it, something happened to pierce her defences. It could be anything from a simple expression or the sight of a blond-haired pregnant woman in the distance. Grief thumped her in the chest with a pain that threatened to overwhelm her.

Pascal took up golf. That's how he coped with the endless pain. Pascal told her it clears his head, makes him appreciate all they have in life. Not Olive. She couldn't figure out how walking around following a little white ball could possibly make her feel any better. In her head, her daughter was stolen from her at a time in her life when she was filled with hope. When Jenny told Olive and Pascal that she was finally pregnant after years of IVF, they were over the moon for her and for James. Every step of the pregnancy was a joy. Olive and Pascal couldn't wait to be grandparents. Jenny was so looking forward to being a mother to her little girl. A sob catches in Olive's throat as, once again, she railed against what happened. In this day and age, she asked herself, how could any fit and healthy woman die in childbirth? It doesn't make sense. How could God be so cruel to take their daughter from them, to take her from the child she loved and yearned for?

"Olive, are you okay?" Sadie laid her hand on Olive's knee.

Olive nodded, unable to speak. She hadn't shared her sorrow with the group. It was Pascal who saw their social media post looking for members and suggested that she might be interested in joining. She had resisted at first but eventually relented two months ago. The meetings were interesting, always fun, and informative. Membership was varied with members of all ages, abilities, and backgrounds. Olive felt like she was just getting to know the others. She found writing therapeutic; putting down on paper her sorrow helped her work her way through it. Olive never shared those pieces with the others, not yet anyway. She possibly never would. It was too raw, too personal. But she enjoyed the free writing in group and reading the work from the other members. Her tentative contributions were always well received. Today she had read her piece out for the first time. The theme was 'An undesirable encounter.' She audibly snorted as her scribbles came back to her, detailing meeting a large dog in the park, off his lead and growling at her. Trying to describe fear was challenging. It was not an emotion she was overly familiar with. Although that encounter couldn't hold a candle to this one.

Olive felt Sadie's hand on hers and opened her eyes. JJ no longer danced around waving a gun. She could hear him muttering behind them. Olive smiled at Sadie. Such a great girl. She reminded her of Jenny. Feisty and brave, ready to conquer the world. Olive said a silent prayer that the world would be a kinder place for Sadie than it was for her darling Jenny. Is this it, she wondered. Is this how I will end my days, a hostage in the library, of all places. The irony of it made her smile.

"Who would have thought of the library as a dangerous place?" she whispered. They all tittered nervously, and Sadie squeezed her hand.

"What's going on?" JJ reappeared, waving the gun around.

"You need to call an ambulance," Sadie stood to face him.

"Shut up and sit down," JJ gestured with the gun.

"And you, young man, need to stop brandishing that gun around."

JJ took several steps back, his eyebrows raised in surprise, but he did lower the gun.

"Sit down, all of you."

Olive opened her mouth to protest but Larry stepped forward and silenced them all.

"It's not open for debate. I want complete silence from you lot. Stay quiet and we'll all get out of here," Larry looked at his watch, "Eighty minutes and we'll all walk out that door."

"But Daniel's in trouble. He can't wait that long," Olive interjected.

"I know. I will get help for him, but I want co-operation from you lot."

Larry went back to the reception desk and lifted the phone.

"DCI Darcy. I figured you were on the line. We have a casualty, nothing too serious. Muppet fell through the ceiling trying to escape."

The room fell silent as they all struggled to hear the one-sided conversation.

"He's conscious but complaining about pain in his ankle. Few cuts and bruises. I'll get him over to the staff exit door. Don't try anything. I have hostages."

Larry strode back into view, pushing the receptionist's chair.

"You," he pointed at Olive, "and you."

He pulled Olive upright and slashed open the duct tape binding her wrists. Olive shook out her wrists and wriggled her fingers, grateful to feel the blood circulating again.

"Let me put some sort of splint on his ankle it before you try to move him," Sadie looked around her frantically for something she could use. She pointed at some shelving sitting beside the staff door, "I can use that and fasten it with duct tape."

With Olive's help, Sadie worked quickly, making Daniel's ankle immobile. JJ and Larry lifted him onto the chair. Daniel winced; his knuckles white as he gripped the arms of the chair. With clenched teeth, he nodded to Sadie.

"It's okay, I'm okay."

"You two," he waved the gun at Olive and Sadie, "wheel him out to the side door, unlock it, and push him outside."

Olive gasped, "We can't push him out. There are steps. The chair will keel over and cause more damage."

"Just do what you're told. Push him out, close the door. I'll be right behind you, and if you hesitate, even for a second, I'll use this," Larry gestured to JJ to give him the gun. JJ giggled nervously and handed to over. Larry pointed it directly at Olive's head.

Chapter 22

Maxwell squinted through his puffed-up eyelids and peered through the floating plaster dust and debris in disbelief at the crumpled body that had fallen through the ceiling.

"Daniel," he whispered, shocked as everyone else in the room was, to see the unexpected reappearance of the one person who held any hope of an early release from their nightmare. JJ poked his ugly head through the hole in the ceiling, a menacing grin on his face.

"Got him, boss," he shouted triumphantly to Larry who was standing beside Daniel. "He knew his number was up, the scumbag."

"Shut up and get down here, you eejit, before you do any more damage," an angry Larry spat out, his mind working overtime on what the fallout would have on their plan to escape.

"Shit, shit, shit," he roared as, fists clenched, he raised his right foot and gave a nearby heavy metal chair an almighty kick sending it careering into the lap of Maxwell, causing him to roar in agony.

"Ah shut up you 'oul fecker," he muttered and turned around to assess the injuries caused to the young lad on the floor. It didn't look good. He was alive but God knows how bad his injuries were. This was all he needed, just when it looked like the Gardai were co-operating.

That JJ was a liability. What had he got himself into. They dragged the injured lad over to the other hostages, but he passed out with the pain.

"Christ almighty." Larry clenched his fists, afraid that he would do serious damage to JJ. They were all talking at him. The women, that pathetic old man, the librarian with the kindly face. That eejit JJ.

"Free her hands. See what she can do for him."

Sadie and Olive gently tended to Daniel as best they could. In the midst of all the panic, they both remained cool and when they saw an opportunity to get the spare keys from the desk they acted quickly. Just as Olive was slipping them into her tunic pocket, Daniel groaned as he regained consciousness.

It's only fair to say that Maxwell felt sympathy for Daniel in his comatose state. In the face of such a dire situation, attitudes can change dramatically. Maxwell's own injuries paled in comparison to what Daniel might be afflicted with and, yes, Maxwell was shocked and unnerved by the turn in events. It slowly dawned on him that his overriding feeling was one of admiration for the young lad's gumption, even if his plan went belly up. He was surprised at his own change of heart towards Daniel.

"He's a plucky young lad," he whispered to Siobhan. "He was obviously trying to get help for us, and he might well have succeeded except for crashing through the ceiling. Must have stood on a spot that couldn't hold his weight."

"It's all so unnecessary," Siobhan moaned quietly. "Why do we do this to one another? Look what this whole disaster has done to Daniel, Maxwell. His life could be ruined, and for what?" she asked rhetorically.

Maxwell felt helpless to comfort her with his back to the wall and hands tied. His back was breaking from sitting on the floor and he could feel the calves of his legs starting to cramp, a situation that occurred usually in the middle of the night when he could get out of bed and stretch his legs until the cramps eased. Now he could do nothing and the toes on his left foot were starting to separate in opposite directions as they cramped. He yelped in pain.

"Sorry, sorry, oh my God I'm in agony," he shouted. "I need to stand up to get rid of this cramp."

JJ came back into the room and, having had a dressing down from Larry and told to go easy on the group, showed a more sympathetic side to his nature. He pulled over a chair and released Maxwell who did a few gyrations with his legs until the pain eased. JJ then barked at him to sit on a chair nearby and he fastened his arms together behind his back.

"Is that better, old man?" he asked gruffly.

"Ah yes, much better and thank you," answered Maxwell, a bit of colour coming back into his messy face. "I'm sorry to cause such a fuss, especially when I see the young lad in such pain but I'm not as fit and able as I used to be. Thank you."

Relief flooded through Maxwell's body at the luxury of sitting upright with his feet on the floor and his back supported by the chair. He watched as Sadie and Olive tended to Daniel who was now conscious and crying in pain. Finally, they lifted him on to an office chair with wheels and pushed him towards an exit.

It was only then Maxwell realised the extent of Daniel's treachery. Maxwell's diary, which had been safely tucked into a zipped pocket in his briefcase, lay on the floor where it had dropped out of Daniel's pocket. Maxwell's entire life, his cowardice and his foolish air of superficial superiority would be laid bare if it got into the wrong hands. It only took a split second for his admiration for Daniel to be replaced by red hot hatred.

Chapter 23

DCI Darcy stood outside at the command post with the armed support team leader, Sergeant Daly, to formulate a plan for breaching the library and safely getting all the hostages out. Sergeant Daly relayed to DCI Darcy a few different plans that he had that might work.

"My first idea is we throw two flash bang grenades in so everyone in the room will be completed disoriented, then a smoke grenade so they can't see us coming," said Sergeant Daly, "I don't want anyone to get hurt so I've opted for my team to use less than lethal beanbag shotguns and taser if necessary."

"Good idea, we don't need extra enquires on top of the one we will have to run into this whole saga," said DCI Darcy. Just then everyone turned to see an ambulance pull up on the street put on standby in case of any injuries.

"Let's pray we don't need the services of these kind men and women," said DCI Darcy. "With my plan, we should catch everyone off guard and hopefully avoid injury. It's better to have them here on scene than not and then someone unfortunately gets shot or stabbed and we have to call them," said Daly.

"Very true, how many men are you going to send in when you breach?" asked DCI Darcy. "My team are extremely highly skilled, and we train for this situation almost daily so I think six should be enough if you agree?"

"Well, there's only two aggressors and you're the expert in this situation so I trust your judgement," said DCI Darcy confidently. The DCI looked around and could see very curious bystanders at the cordon wondering what was happening inside. Darcy was just glad nobody else has wandered in and become part of this big mess before first responders arrived. He decided to call again to gauge what kind of atmosphere was inside now. When he finally got through, JJ answered the phone abruptly.

"What do you want," he said with venom.

"I was just wondering is everyone ok in there.

"Yea everyone is ok apart from one idiot who tried to escape through the roof and fell."

"Ok well we need to get him out then as soon as possible, we have ambulances outside, you can drop him at the door, and we will stay back."

There was silence on the line for a few seconds and then JJ finally said, "I'll ask the boss and I'll be back."

He left the line open while he went to consult with the ringleader and Darcy listened intensely to see could he hear any other noise on the line. He couldn't hear anything at all so the hostages must have been in another room.

JJ came back on the phone, "Ok the boss has agreed but he said if you try any sneaky moves to get in, he will put a bullet in one of the hostages, got it?" JJ said with authority.

"We won't try anything; our priority is to help anyone who is sick or injured. Let me know when you're coming so I can get my team to retreat back," said Darcy.

After about 5 minutes, JJ came back on the phone. "Ok we are letting him out now. As I said u try anything and one of them dies."

Chapter 24

Siobhan practised her deep breathing, the method she used to calm herself when that niggly flutter of nervous tension hit her stomach. Her usual calm exterior belied what was going on side. She hadn't wanted to show her fear to JJ when he pushed her along the corridor in search of the source of the sneeze. When she opened the door to the office and saw the vent hanging loose, and the dust on the desk underneath, she had tried to back out so JJ wouldn't see it, but he was right behind her, and she was powerless to stop him. It was obvious that someone had climbed into the roof space through the air vent. It's a pity he hadn't thought to close it after him. It was a sure-fire giveaway to his whereabouts.

"What the…" he shoved her, and she stumbled forward, scraping her hip painfully on the door handle. Siobhan yelped then cowered as JJ lifted his fist. The blow caught her on her shoulder sending her sprawling to the floor. Dazed, she stayed there, anxious to avoid another blow. JJ paid no attention to her. He was focused on climbing from the top of the desk into the roof space. At the sight of his denim-clad legs swinging overhead as he hoisted himself up, she dragged herself out into the corridor and into the storeroom.

Her left hip and shoulder were throbbing as she studied the room for a place to hide. In the corner stood an old-fashioned book trolley, the type they used on the old library buses. It was an antique really and she wondered why it would be stored here of all places when it should be in a museum. It looked exactly like the one her grandmother had told her about. She had been a librarian in Kerry and spent years in the mobile library. They travelled all around the county visiting schools and hospitals and all sorts of places. During transit the books were stored inside the trolley. It looked like a box on wheels but when they reached their destination it converted into a mobile bookshelf. The sides were hinged and once opened and locked in place revealed shelving twice the height of the original box with thin shelves just the right width for books. Ingenious really, she thought, and hopefully somewhere I can hide until I figure out what to do.

It was a tight squeeze, but she managed it. The uproar was continuing in the main area of the building. Closing her mind to what was going on around her she practised her breathing. In for three, hold for three, out for three. Gently, quietly, methodically. Siobhan tried to drag herself into the present but the trauma of what happened to her all those years ago was reignited the second she closed the door. Breath Siobhan, in for three, hold for three, out for three but her usual trick wasn't enough to banish the clawing blackness invading her.

She found herself right back to 10-year-old Siobhan, locked in the cubby hole, blindfolded and scared. That voice came back to haunt her. Gravelly, disembodied, for she never saw him, never got to put a face to the voice. Is that why it still haunted her? Years of therapy never managed to answer that question for her. The same therapy helped that voice slowly disappear from her brain, only reappearing in moments of extreme stress. Like now, in the darkness, waiting for some sort of harm to befall her.

Siobhan burst out of the box, gasping for breath, fear clasping her chest in a tight, twisted knot. On the edge of her consciousness, she could hear the shouting from the main library. Its presence snapped her mind back to the present and the danger she was in. Judging by the shouts and screams echoing from the main library area, Daniel had been found and Larry wasn't too happy about it.

Breathe Siobhan, she told herself, repeating the manta over and over, breathe in for three, hold for three, breath out for three, until she felt her heart rate return to normal. It was time to formulate an escape plan before they twigged that she was missing and came looking for her. This could be their last chance to get help and it was down to her. Siobhan could never imagine herself as a natural leader. She was a team player, happy to give her utmost to the team but always in the background. That's where she was happiest. She could apply herself, fulfil her image of a conscientious, hard-working young woman who never got stressed or uptight. Good in a crisis, problem solver, that's what was printed on her LinkedIn profile. Most of the time, that was correct, at least outwardly. Inside she felt like a swan, calm exterior, paddling like mad underneath to keep it all together.

Mentally she pulled herself upright, starting with her toes, she stretched to her full height, feeling her confidence grow exponentially. Dismay temporarily clouded her resolve when she saw the state of her clothes. Her pristine navy skirt was smeared with cobwebs, her suede heels scuffed. Brushing away the bulk of the damage with her hands she laughed to herself, feeling strangely maniacal. Get a grip, Siobhan, she told herself, find a way out before it's too late.

Using the noise in the main library area to mask her movements, Siobhan left the storeroom and continued down the corridor. It was a staff area, closed to the public so she had no idea what was there. A door to her left opened into what looked like a small storage room. It was dark but some sliver of light caught her eye as the door opened and disappeared as she stood there in the opening. Was there a window? Did the breeze from opening the door reveal something but it fluttered back in place? Siobhan's curiosity aroused; she stepped inside. Shelves filled the room from left to right, stacked with boxes of stationary and used tins of pain. There was a ladder perched against the wall behind one set of shelves. Paint splattered dust sheets hung from the top rung of the ladder. Siobhan squeezed her way past the shelves and pushed aside the dust sheet.

She couldn't believe her eyes. A door. Her heart raced. The door was obviously unused, possibly never opened. She tried the handle. Locked, of course, it's locked, muppet, she thought as her heart rate went back to normal. As she dropped the dust sheet back into its original place, she saw it. A key, hanging on a hook on the left side of the door frame. Siobhan listened intently. The ongoing commotion hadn't abated, and she knew it was only a matter of time before JJ realised she was missing. She tried the key in the lock and couldn't believe her good luck when it engaged. She turned the handle and pushed. The door stuck but she was sure it was down to years of accumulated dust, rather than any failure of the locking mechanism to engage. Siobhan put her full weight against the door and pushed again. With a stubborn creak the door opened, and Siobhan found herself in a dark yard, totally enclosed with high steel fencing.

Siobhan couldn't control the sob that escaped her. Just when she thought she was free, she ended up here. It was a cage of some sort, built around a defunct oil tank, rusted as if abandoned years ago. No lights, muffled sound. She tried to figure out where it was situated. Surely the Gardai had the building surrounded but this cage appeared to be tucked away behind an annexe of the building. She looked back towards the open door. What should she do? Go back and look for another way to escape? Or stay here. She couldn't risk shouting for help, in case they heard her. Dithering, she paced two steps forward, two steps back. Decision made; she went back inside leaving the door open. Maybe if they came looking for her, they would think she escaped out that way and she could stay free long enough to be of some use to the others.

Chapter 25

"What's this?" said JJ picking Maxwell's diary off the floor and tossing it around in the air. He caught it on its third summersault and flicked it open.

"Well, well, well. Listen up to this. 'When I walked out of the bank on my final day I was crippled with shame. I hadn't done the right thing. I panicked. Looking back, I am appalled at my cowardice and wish I had acted differently. The loss of respect from my colleagues has clung to me like a bad smell. I have lost everything. My family don't want to know me, and my marriage is over. I wonder is it work carrying on.'

Maxwell groaned. It was plain for all to see his humiliation at hearing his dark and private thoughts being laid bare in front of everyone. He blinked rapidly trying to force back his tears.

"Give it to me, please," he pleaded with JJ.

It was excruciating for the group to witness his distress, so they averted their eyes, mostly towards JJ as if pleading for him to give it a rest.

"Now isn't that interesting? You're a fucking coward, aren't ya, ya big sissy."

Sadie bravely intervened, much to everyone's relief.

"Leave him alone. He's not a coward. You may not know it but we're a creative writer's group so what we write is straight out of our imagination. What you're reading is fiction, isn't that right Maxwell?"

Maxwell was too shocked to answer. He realised that Sadie was offering him a way to save his image, showing a maturity way beyond her years. He knew he couldn't respond without losing all control. His head dropped as if a puppeteer had suddenly loosened the string that held it steady, and his chin flopped on his chest. Despite his best attempt to restrain them, tears streamed down his face.

JJ flipped through another few pages and started to read aloud again in plaintive tones.

"I've lost everything now and I've nothing left to live for," JJ read. "Boo, hoo, hoo. What a baby!"

There was a shocked silence. Nobody knew what to say but waves of sympathy and embarrassment at Maxwell's predicament were palpable. Except for JJ, who ploughed on regardless.

"So, you're not much better than me, are ya? Letting people down when they looked up to you? You're a sad fucker." He flung the diary at Maxwell, the pages fluttering as it landed on the ground in front of him.

Sadie had had enough of this shit. She was spitting fire.

"You can talk JJ! Look at yourself, jeering and maiming an elderly man who didn't do you any harm. Who's the coward here?"

"It's all right, Sadie. He's right. I am a coward," whispered Maxwell.

"No, Maxwell, we all make mistakes and you've paid dearly for yours. That's just life. You make mistakes because you're human and you try to put things right if you can. But it's people who make mistakes and never learn that what they're doing is evil and bad that are the real cowards!" she glared at JJ.

"Shut your face or I'll shut it for ya!" JJ snapped back at her.

"Go on, do it JJ. My god, what would your mother and father think of you now? You know, everyone in the parish was so proud of you when you were boxing. The whole town looked up to you, you were so fit and dedicated. You were a role model for all the young lads in the area. Now look at yourself. You're a shambles and you're trying to make yourself be a 'Big Man' by picking on an elderly man. You should be ashamed of yourself."

JJ kicked a chair and set it careering across the room.

"Ah, fuck off you. Look at you now! You're not so great now, are ya?"

Those words, while directed at Sadie, lingered in Maxwell's head. He was not so great now. In fact, he hadn't been great for so long that he had lost sight of the last time he felt good about himself. Depression was his daily – and nightly - companion. Suicidal thoughts were never far from the surface and increasingly he saw taking his own life as a way to end all the wracking pain in his heart. Who would give a damn? Nobody, not one person.

Some days he didn't get out of bed or draw the curtains. The only bright spot in his long dreary days was coming to the writing group and that had become a struggle, pretending, faking it. He was a sham, and he was weary of playing these stupid games. He was beyond weary.

Images flickered through his mind of one dismal night last week when he had driven to the river. He knew the exact spot where the current of the river was fast, and it was deep. He parked in a quiet spot where very few people passed and took his phone out of his pocket. He opened his contacts and flicked through them. Should he send a goodbye message to his son and daughter? He hadn't been in touch for years, why should he burden them now?

As he scrolled further, he came across a number for Samaritans which he didn't remember putting on his phone. He knew it was a confidential helpline for people in distress and while he desperately needed someone to talk to what would he say? He didn't have words for how he felt. He had a vague memory of hearing a Samaritan volunteer being interviewed on the radio. He must have put the Freephone number into his contacts list then. He remembered her saying that Samaritans were there to offer emotional support and to listen, not to judge. Tentatively, he pressed his finger on the contact, and it rang for a few seconds.

"You're through to Samaritans. My name is Gerry. How can I help you?"

The voice was soft and welcoming. Maxwell couldn't answer but he didn't hang up. The voice on the other end of the phone assured him there was no rush, that he would stay on the line as long as he needed. He understood how difficult it might be to talk when life got too much and explained how it can help to talk about how you feel.

'Just take your time. We're not here to judge and it can help to get dark thoughts out in the open. You're not alone.'

That phrase 'you're not alone' was the undoing of Maxwell that night. He started to sob aloud, desperate to reach out and unburden himself.

Maxwell had no concept of time during that call, but he knew he eventually was able to say a few words and those words became a torrent of emotion that poured out, of his isolation, his loneliness, his despair. For the first time ever, he was honest about his feelings. "I can't go on; I want to end it and I don't know how or if I could be happy again. I've burnt so many bridges and hurt so many people."

He was offered a call back the following day which he gladly accepted. Turning the car for home Maxwell felt exhausted but he also knew that opening up to Samaritans had helped him survive that night. He had spoken to them several times since.

And now, only a few days since the last call, he was in this life-threatening situation, a situation beyond his control.

Sadie was keeping an eye on Maxwell. She looked over and smiled at him when she caught his eye, trying to give him a little boost, to let him know she was on his side.

Maxwell didn't seem to notice. The good vibes weren't hitting home as his thoughts had veered down a different path. A 'nothing to lose' path, one he knew so well, but a tiny glimmer flickered in his mind. He badly needed to do something, anything, that would jolt him out of his misery.

"I want to talk to Larry," he said to JJ with what little authority he could muster. "Could you ask him to come in here or let me go to him. I'm deadly serious about this."

Larry walked into the room at that moment.

"What's going on here? What have you been up to JJ?"

"He wants to speak to you," said JJ pointing to Maxwell. There was a bit of to-ing and fro-ing and after a few minutes Larry, who was shocked at the state of Maxwell up close, agreed to speak to him in private. He led the way into the corridor and shut the door behind Maxwell. He pulled over a chair for him to sit on.

"OK. What do you want to say? Make it quick. I don't have time for messing about, so it better be good."

Maxwell took a deep breath and looked Larry straight in the eyes.

He set out a proposal that the rest of the group should be released, and they should take him as a sole hostage.

"Listen to me. You have nothing to gain by keeping everyone captive when you could just hold me. You'd gain sympathy if you showed some humanity to the rest of the group. I'll speak up for you if push comes to shove and say you treated us fairly."

Larry listened and seemed to be weighing up what was said, so Maxwell continued.

"I don't know what's behind all this, and I don't want to know, but what I do know is that if it comes to a shoot-out, one dead body is better than five. And I'm an old man, I've lived my life. The others are younger with responsibilities, as you'll know all about that very soon when your son or daughter is born."

Larry said nothing.

"You're in over your head, Larry, and the Gardai have the place surrounded. Don't blow it. You'll regret it for the rest of your life."

Chapter 26

"We have movement at the side exit, it looks like the door is opening" came a static voice across Ciaran's radio.

The message was redundant as Ciaran could see the door opening himself, but it was good police protocol. Clicking on his own radio he spoke.

"Hold steady, no one move without the order."

The door opened and a man in an office chair was pushed out. Even from a distance behind his car Ciaran could see there was something wrong with the man from the awkward way he sat in his chair. This was clear when the chair hit the bottom of the ramp and tipped forward dumping the man on the ground. An ear-splitting shriek erupted from the man as he struggled on the ground. In a break between screams as the man ran out of air Ciaran heard his phone ringing. Pulling it out of his pocket, he saw it was the library. How was he going to hear anything over the screaming? Ominously, just then the screaming stopped, but at least he would hear the call.

"Detective Chief Inspector Darcy speaking."

As he spoke Ciaran saw Olive and another young lady come out and start dragging the man back in. By his silence and the limp way, he flopped about as they pulled him, he was clearly unconscious. Ciaran heard the phone creak in his ear as he watched Olive and he realised he was going to crush his phone if he didn't get a grip of himself. Remember your training, the voice in his head said.

"I mean business Inspector. I didn't even touch that fucker, but just imagine if I had. Where is my transport?"

"How do you expect me to have it here already? It will be here; I have another 40 minutes. Where do you want it to take you?"

"Fuck off. So, you can prepare the way for me? Look that idiot injured himself, but he is staying in here. You can either leave him or send in a medic. Also, I am hungry, send in some Domino's. I want the works."

"Ok, ok. I will send in a medic, but would it not be easier just leave him out here for us to look after? Work with me here, how many hostages have you still in there? Surely, they are enough?"

"He stays. Don't fuck with me.'

"Ok I will send in a medic; it will take me a few minutes to get organised. Do you want the medic in the front door or the side door?"

"Side door. And no messing around, the medic comes in underwear only and all his gear in a see-through bag. You will not fuck me."

"Ok, it will take time to organise. I will ring you back on this line when we are ready to go in. Domino's, work with me here Larry. How much do you want, how many do I order for? I will rush it through, but it will take time. How do you suppose I can do this quickly; its Derby Day remember?"

"The works for eight, and make sure there is ketchup, and none of that own brand shite."

The line went dead in Ciaran's hand as the two women struggled with getting the man back inside the door.

Ciaran went rigid and threw his head in the air. He really wanted to smash his phone on the ground, but his men were watching. Lead by example, he said to himself if I lose it then things will quickly escalate into shots and death. Pulling himself together Ciaran started flicking through a mental roster of available medics. This guy was good, he was screwing Ciaran good. Ciaran would have to give him another hostage, when the medic entered the building. Not, only that, the medic would have to go in half naked. Better make it a male medic, no need to add more controversy by offering a half nude female.

Chapter 27

Back inside, at the side exit Olive was shaking with rage. Her early fear had passed, and her blood was up again. If she had the strength and agility of even ten years ago, she would take on this thug, but she had promised Ciaran. She could be overly optimistic on some things. Tackling a man half her age was not one of those things. Anyway, she knew that Ciaran would regret her making such a foolish play even if she happened to live through it.

She still had a few brain cells that were not consumed by rage at the way they had been forced to manhandle poor Daniel. She could only hope that JJ mistook her shaking for fear rather than rage. Just don't make eye contact, she thought.

The tangy scent of urine cut through some of her rage. It was hard to tell if it was from Daniel or Sadie. Daniel had passed out from the pain and for his sake Olive hoped he would stay that way until they could get him help. Sadie looked like she was going to follow Daniel into unconsciousness if something wasn't done soon. Putting an extra tremble into her voice, Olive said.

"Please, can you pull him back, he is far too heavy for us. Otherwise, you will have to carry all three of us back inside."

Grunting, JJ grabbed Daniels arm from Sadie and dragged him along the ground. Olive dropped Daniels's arm as he was pulled forward and slid her arm around Sadie.

"We will get through this," she whispered and gave Sadie's waist a slight squeeze. Olive felt a slight squeeze on her shoulder in return from Sadie. Maybe Sadie isn't in as bad a shape as she looks, thought Olive.

JJ pushed his way back through the fire door and dumped Daniel in a pile.

Olive could see that the group was as they had left them. Larry was pacing around on his mobile phone. He was clearly not happy about something, but Olive had no idea what he might look like happy.

"That's not the deal." He said voice rising as he clenched and unclenched his fist. "The deal was two hours."

There was silence as he listened and continued to pace. JJ watched him intently.

"Fuck that! We had a deal; you can't go changing it now," Larry was screaming down the phone.

"What is going on Larry?" JJ demanded striding forward.

"Shut up," he said, waving JJ away.

"No, no, not you. I meant this idiot here." There was another pause, followed by Larry saying, "Ok I am listening."

Olive didn't bother listening any further. Giving Sadie another gentle squeeze on the waist she started backing the two of them into the fire door. Thankfully the fire door swung both ways and bless Sadie's heart she kept her nerve and silently followed Olive.

Back at the side exit Sadie dared a whisper.

"What are we doing, it is locked."

"I have the key remember."

Digging in her pockets Olive came out with the spare key from the library desk. Holding it up triumphantly she gave herself a moment to savour it and then slid the key into the lock.

It slid into the lock without issue, but it wouldn't turn. It must have been cut off the master key but wasn't a perfect copy. Olive tried to jimmy it back and forth to get through the tumblers, but it wouldn't turn.

She could feel the pressure mounting as the seconds swept past and the key didn't turn. Sadie was a fireball presence of tension and expectation that almost broke Olive's composure.

What to do now? Olive thought. 'Keep trying the lock and risk getting caught here? Try the back door and get caught there? Try hide in the limited space in the library? That hadn't work well for her or Daniel. Go back and hope no one noticed they had been missing? All bad options.'

Chapter 28

Betty sat tied and uncomfortable in her place of work, with a group of people she barely knew, and two thugs she didn't know at all. The situation brought anxiety and anger to the pit of her stomach. Being forced to stay at her workplace well past finishing time angered her even more.

As the minutes ticked by, Betty thought she could reason with Larry and JJ to give up their asinine antics and release everyone. Thinking of where she should be right now, if the two captors had not forced their way into the library. Bloody heck, she whispered to herself as Betty noted 5:30pm beaming from the large clock on the wall. Proudly it displayed time like a Las Vegas neon sign. Mother will be needing her dinner and medication shortly. She will be so angry with me if I'm late, she thought.

Mulling over what she might say to her captors of her mother's dependence on her. After all she is 80 years old. Would they listen? Would they have empathy? Would they let her go? Lots of questions but just one realistic answer came to mind.

In a dream like state of reverie, Betty allowed her mind to drift to the years growing up with her mother. God knows they hadn't been easy. Her counsellors' words were talking to her inner voice. "Your mother has controlled your every move, word, even thoughts since you were born. It's time to take control of your own mind." She felt her anxiety and anger abating. From the first meeting with the counsellor unbeknown to her mother, Betty learned how to control and maintain rational, reasonable thinking, regardless of her mother's controlling ways.

Angela Costello was a blow in from the next county once she married Betty's father. Her parents owned and ran the newsagents after Betty's paternal Grandparents died. Angela was a very proud woman in her day, always believed the patrons of their shop were beneath her. She had airs and graces above her station and no matter the circumstances, both her husband and young Betty had to conform to her way in order to impress the locals. By the time Betty was sixteen years old she learned life was easier if she went along with her mother's demands rather than rocking the boat. Her father too had learned to conform shortly after marrying Angela. He did so for two reasons, the first, he was a God fearing catholic and the commandment of 'Thou shalt not kill' was never far from his mind. The second reason was for a quiet life. As the years passed, Tom Costello was brow-beaten more and more by Angela, she had both Tom and Betty well under her thumb.

Tom spent a lot of time in his daughters' company, believing this was the only way he could protect his daughter from her mother's wrath. Tears came to Betty's eyes, as she remembered the kindhearted, gentle soul, her father. It had been him who had the most compassion for Betty. She remembered an evening as they sat by the river talking about her schoolwork. Betty expressed how happy she would be when she finished secondary and moved away to college. Free from her mothers' control and constant criticism.

With an angelic yet sad smile, her father placed his comforting hand on her cheek, saying, "sorry my child, as long as there is a breath in your mother's body she will control you, if you let her."

That summer while waiting for the results of her leaving cert and a college place, Betty secured a summer job in the 'Tea Rooms' with John and Mary Berns. John had attended school with Tom, and they had remained friends, despite Angela expressing her disapproval. John and Mary Berns did not have the 'class' that Angela desired.

Due to Angela's mean and controlling ways, Tom knew Angela would expect her daughter to hand over her wage packet from the tea rooms each week. Tom was not a deceitful man but being married to Angela all these years he knew nothing she did or said would surprise him. So, Tom asked Mary Berns if she would divide Betty's wages into two envelopes each Friday. The first for Betty to present to her mother, the second, was for Betty to squirrel away for her future.

"Ok, hand it over. You hardly think we're going to feed you for free my dear." Her mother would announce each pay day as Betty walked through the door. Reluctantly, Betty handed over the small sealed brown envelope. As she turned away from her mother, a quick glance at her father was rewarded with a wink and a loving smile. Feeling quite elated Betty prayed her mother would not learn of the second envelope with the remainder of her wages. The secret portion of money empowered Betty as she got emotionally stronger to deal with her mother.

Betty knew her parents had saved for her college education. The funds were in a bank account in her mother's sole name. Angela had it imbedded in both the mind of her husband and daughter, that she would drip feed the money to the College as required, and neither of them had to concern themselves further.

Her mothers' control over Betty and her father, both financial and every aspect of their daily lives was becoming more apparent to Betty the older she became.

One day, Dear God, one day, I'll be free financially and emotionally from my mother's control, she thought. But for now, she had to conform for her and her father's sake.

Chapter 29

"Who the fuck was that?" JJ asked again as he squared up to Larry.

Taking a deep breath with his eyes closed Larry patted the air.

"Relax man. Plans have changed that's all."

"There is still a plan? JJ asked "The only plan I see is plan F. We are fucked."

"Chill, I'll explain. Go check those guys are still tied up first." Said Larry.

"What about the guy over by the door?"

"Is he dead?"

"No just unconscious I think."

"Then just drag him over beside the others," said Larry. "Wait first give me that gun."

JJ hesitated but then handed over the gun.

Larry looked down at his phone again while JJ went to check the hostages. The screen lit up and messages flashed on the screen in quick succession but Larry's hand shock too violently to be able to make out the blurred words. He quickly stuffed the phone into his pocket. In his other hand the solid grip of the gun imprinted its crosshatch pattern into his skin as he squeezed. Needing movement, he walked over to the corner away from the group on the floor. The walls were covered in bookshelves full of children's books. Damp sweat bloomed on Larry's forehead as he took in the brightly coloured book spines. Leaning a shoulder against the books he closed his eyes.

"One Marie, two Marie, three Marie, four Marie" he gasped while breathing in.

"One Marie, two Marie, three Marie, four Marie" he repeated while holding his breath.

"One Marie, two Marie, three Marie, four Marie" he said on last time breathing out.

Larry then opened his eyes and his hand only tremored slightly as he took his phone back out. Once more the screen flashed displaying 13 missed calls and 27 unread messages, all from Marie and silenced because of his phone settings for today.

The latest message from Marie had only four pitiful words:

Please, I need you.

Larry flicked his thumb across the screen scanning through the texts. Some were a few words like her last and other's paragraphs long, they covered everything violence and abuse to love and forgiveness. But the message was clear, his son was on his way, and he was not there for him. Like father like son it seemed, they would each follow their own plan and the consequences be damned.

"So, explain this fucking genius plan?" JJ asked pulling Larry out of his phone.

Locking his phone screen Larry turned to JJ.

"Do you know The Carpenter? asked Larry.

"The Carpenter? Of course I know of The Carpenter. Who doesn't? I have never met him through," JJ added quickly.

"Yea, well, it is through him that we got this job."

"Fuck off."

"Yea, his guys gave me the set up for this," said Larry.

"I thought it was weird that you came with me on this job, but gift horse and all that. Well, we are really fucked now. We didn't get enough from that bookies to cover what he will want as his cut?"

"That's the thing, JJ, what we got from the bookies was to be a bonus, the real job was to create trouble for the cops. But The Carpenter got wind of the fact that we are holed up here, and he wants us to keep the cops here for three hours."

"Fuuuck," said JJ.

They both jumped as the shrill tones of the library phone rang out.

Stomping over Larry grabbed the handset almost knocking the phone stand off the table.

"What?"

"Hi Larry, its Ciaran here again. I have that medic ready to go in, his name in Brendan. How are you doing in there?"

"Send him in when you see me at the door," said Larry and hung up before Ciaran could say more.

"It's the medic, go let him in," said Larry. "And here, take the knife".

"Make sure you search him and that he has no weapons or needles," Larry called after JJ as he headed for the door.

The guilty weight of unanswered messages in his pocket called to Larry as he glanced over at the hostages. They all seemed sufficiently browbeaten; some were whispering but none dared make eye contact as his hand found his pocket.

He then froze. Where was the blonde? Where was the rest? There was only four. Three? There should be seven or was it eight, six?? Either way some were missing.

Larry ran over to the door, putting his back to the bookshelves so he would be behind the door when it opened. He tried to settle his breathing again as he squeezed the handle of the gun in both hands close to his chest.

His heart beat out a staccato rhythm as he waited. A single drop of sweat run a line of tickles down his chest from his armpit, but he didn't dare move.

Finally, the door opened, and an average man covered in coarse black body hair wearing only Homer Simpsons boxers and grey socks walked in, followed closely by JJ.

Larry sprang forward from his hiding place and hammered the man in the back of the neck with the butt of the gun. He fell into a heap on top of his medical bag.

"What the," started JJ.

"Shut up," Larry snarled. "Some of them escaped. These bastards got some of them out". Larry pointed the gun down at the prone medic to make it absolutely clear which bastards he was talking about. As he pointed his finger squeezed.

A crack of gunfire shattered the bruised and battered tranquillity the library once had.

Chapter 30

Siobhan had barely stepped back inside the room when she heard the bang. She froze, uncertain on the origin. Was it inside or outside the building? Had someone tried to escape? The hair stood on the back of her neck. A lone sliver of sweat trickled down her back. She listened intently as muffled shouting echoed from the main room. She felt some sort of movement to her right and whipped her head around. Relief flooded through her at the sight of Sadie and Olive, both with their figures to their lips gesturing silence.

"This way," Siobhan whispered, bringing them outside, "but can't escape this way. It leads nowhere." She quickly told the two women anxious not to raise their hopes.

"We need a plan," Olive said. "Quickly before they come looking for us. Are you sure there's no exit from here?"

"Positive," Siobhan said. "I think there's another exit back along the corridor to the left. There has to be a fire exit."

"I think we should split up," Olive took charge. "At least then if they catch one of us, it might distract them long enough for the others to get help."

"I'll go first," Sadie said. "I'll go back the way we came. Maybe we missed something."

"I don't think we missed anything," Olive said. "We'll go the other way. We have the option then to split up if we need to. Siobhan, will

129

you check this area again. There has to be an exit or some way of getting over that fence."

The two women crept out the door into the corridor, any noise masked by the commotion coming from the main library. Once again Siobhan searched every inch of the yard for some sort of exit. Nothing. The yard didn't make sense. Why was there no way in or out? She knew the building was an annexe to the old library built back in the 30's and it in turn was built on the site of the old British barracks. God knows what the original layout was. She wondered if there were old tunnels, their entrances blocked, or unused for so long that they were forgotten about. She stepped back inside the room and scoured every corner looking for anything out of the ordinary.

This room was in the middle of refurbishment and the floor had been lifted to reveal old pine floorboards, partially rotten in places. Although Siobhan thought it was odd that they would leave all those boxes of files in the room if they intended to replace the floor. Surely, they would have been cleared out and stored elsewhere. She looked closer at the pile of boxes and shelving. The bookshelves were set out from the wall. Several boxes blocked the gap, but Siobhan guessed the space was big enough to hide behind if those crooks came looking for her. Looking around her, she spotted a stool in the corner. Lifting it carefully she placed it in front of the pile of boxes. She listened, afraid that those men would hear movement and come looking for her. It was okay for Olive to talk about finding an exit, breaking out, getting help. That's how Olive is. Brave, outspoken, a force to be reckoned with.

Siobhan was more accustomed to blending into the background. She had years of training. As a child she learned how to stay as quiet as a church mouse when her father went on a rampage. When he died it was a relief, as much for Siobhan as for her mother. That fall down the stairs was a blessing in disguise, although for years afterwards her dreams were haunted by a fleeting glimpse of her mother at the top of the stairs with her palms outstretched as her father roared before crashing against the glass at the bottom of the stairs. Siobhan never told her mother what she saw from her hiding place in the airing cupboard. She never told anybody. That secret she would take with her to the grave. Which could be coming sooner than she anticipated if she didn't find somewhere to hide.

Standing on top of the stool gave her just enough height to reach up and carefully pull one of the boxes towards her. Siobhan braced herself to support the weight, then gave a sigh of relief when it was manageable. Siobhan listened again. All good. Carefully she lifted down two more boxes. She could see over the remaining tower into the space between the bookshelves and the wall. The perfect den. Boxes were stacked in two more rows, but not as high. She could climb in and move some boxes to the outside, leaving her safe, hidden from view, until Olive or Sadie found help.

Chapter 31

Olive followed Sadie back out into the hall. She was impressed with Sadie's confidence as she led the way or was it just ignorance that helped her put one foot in front of the other in search of an exit. The bang they had just heard before finding Siobhan was unmistakably small arms fire. A single shot like that didn't mean rescue only trouble. The kidnappers were either losing control or purposefully raising the stakes. Olive wasn't sure at this point which was worse.

The swish of the fire door opening as Sadie pushed her way into the next room down the hall sounded loud in Olives ears but then again so did her breathing. It was all thanks to the adrenaline cocktail she had running through her. Olive squeezed into the room after Sadie and let the fire door slide closed on its own. Olive hated fire doors, of course she understood the importance but why did they all have to be so heavy and damned ugly. They were especially ugly when retrofitted into old building like this one. Glancing around the room Olive saw more of the clash of modern and traditional. The room was some type of back office with books of all shapes and size cluttered among utilitarian desks and floating shelves. The decorative coving in the ceiling was battling for the memories of what once was in the room, and the off white wooden framed windows were making a last stand against the modern black external security bars.

"Another dead end," said Sadie, as a small note of desperation caught the end of her sentence.

"Don't be too quick to judge my dear. This is an old building, and like most of us of the older vintage, we can be slow to give up our secrets."

"But the windows are barred, and the only door is the one we came in. I don't think there are any secrets in this room. This isn't like one of those spy stories you write. We can't just write in a miraculous escape," Sadie said with a weak smile.

"If only it was one of my stories, I would show those buffoons out there a thing or two. Forget an escape, they would be begging for one."

This strengthens Sadie's smile a little but like an engine running on fumes it quickly spluttered out.

'This wasn't always a library, and it was built during the time when big attics and cellars were a standard in state buildings. Let's see if we can't find a trap down somewhere, the best bet is to try and feel for a draught," said Olive.

"I don't want to go into the attic, not after what happened to poor Daniel. So, let's hope for a cellar. I'll start over here."

On hands and knees, they each crawled around the desks and chairs trying to feel for a draught or a cut in the threadbare carpet that didn't match. Olive felt vulnerable on her knees, and she knew they were highly unlikely to find anything but at least it kept Sadie occupied while she tried to think.

But her mind wandered and rather than strategizing on how to best help Tom or stop this herself she was wondering and not for the first time was there something more than just friendship between Sadie and Daniel. Sadie was always very complimentary of Daniel's writing in the group and beamed when he returned the compliments. Then again, they were both positive about everyone writing. Well, everyone but Maxwell. Daniel seemed to spin a negative impression of Maxwell's writing without explicitly saying it was bad. Male ego, nothing but trouble!

Sadie was very concerned when Daniel fell through the ceiling, natural of course. Was it more than just the concern of a kind-hearted friend Olive wondered? Then again was Olive just trying to play match maker for two young hearts whether they wanted it or not. Elders were great at pushing romance as an obvious solution to independent youth as if it was a problem that needed solving. Olive had cursed this very attitude in her own youth and dodged many the inconvenient match.

"I found no secrets on my side, how about you Olive?" Sadie asked as she got to her feet.

"Nothing either. Let's try the writing room while we can. I never noticed anything on the floor in there but then again, I never looked either."

"Let's hope there is," said Sadie. "Unless here is a magic portal in the bathroom there are no other rooms to check."

With determination Sadie led the way as they snuck back out and down the hall into the writing room. Once in the room with the door safely closed Sadie took a deep breath as if she was about to take a plunge and squared up to Olive.

"What do you think that loud bang was just before we found Siobhan," Sadie said in a rush.

The truth was the best approach here Olive thought as she gently took Sadie's hand.

"That was a gunshot my dear".

"No, are you sure," Sadie said. Like a balloon quickly losing air, the confidence drained from Sadie and her posture slumped.

"Positive."

Sadie's perfectly long eyelashes flickered as her hazel eyes bulged in realisation.

"Not Daniel?" Sadie whispered. Olive lip read what she said the words barely making it past Sadie's lips.

"Oh no, I am sure he is fine dear. I am sure it was just a warning shot and nothing more. I am sure he is safe." Olive said, sometimes too much truth is a bad thing.

"How can you be sure?"

"Those guys out there are amateurs, but they know enough to know that if they seriously harm any of us there will be no escape for them."

Sadie clung to this answer, the alterative was too much to think about. Seeing that Sadie was seriously shaken and had been ignorant of the gunshot, Olive suggested they sit on the floor together for a minute.

"Why don't we talk about something else?" Said Olive as they settled on the floor. "How is that sweet dog of yours, Benji?"

Sadie's hazel eyes bulged once again; this time she gasped a breath deep into her lungs. Olive knew this air had to go somewhere and did the only thing she could. She clamped her hand down on Sadie's open mouth and with her iron grip grabbed the back of her head, as her weight fell on Sadie, they both tumbled flat on the floor.

Chapter 32

DCI Darcy and his team were standing outside the library when they heard a sudden and very loud bang. Everybody instinctively knew it was a gunshot.

"Shit, I hope that was only a warning shot," DCI Darcy said to himself. He picked up his radio. "Everyone hold your position," he said forcefully.

Tension spread like wildfire as each person wondered what was going to happen next. Darcy was hastily hammering out their next move with the firearms team leader when his phone rang. It was his superior.

"What can I do for you, boss?"

"Darcy. I think there's a leak in the team."

"Well, it's not bloody well me," Darcy protested, his tone irate and he paced up and down.

"I know that, Darcy. I have absolute faith in you, but the powers that be don't know…"

"Listen, there's been a shot fired. I haven't time for this right now."

"Right," said Superintendent O'Shea. "That's a major escalation."

The line went quiet. Darcy could practically hear the cogs turning in the superintendent's brain.

"Listen, I'm going to send an external observer. That'll keep the top brass off my neck and give you time to find this leak."

"Yes sir, thank you Sir," Darcy said before hanging up. "This is all I fucking need now." He rubbed his hand over his mouth in frustration before calling over the firearms team leader, Sergeant Daly.

"There's a new external DCI coming, the super thinks there's been an internal leak." As the words left his mouth, he suddenly wondered if he should have said anything to another officer.

The surprise on Sgt Daly's face was genuine. "You're joking," he said with a groan, his eyes flickering around the gathering. "Okay, from now on we just communicate between ourselves, everyone else just gets orders, it's the best way to go in case the super is right, and it is someone on the team."

***

Back at the station, Superintendent O'Shea sat at his desk in a big comfortable black leather chair, wondering where the leak could have come from and irate that someone could disrespect their position in this way. He stood and walked over to his coffee maker to get a fresh cup while he waited on the replacement DCI to report to him for exact instructions on how to manage the scene. The situation was bad enough without having to root out a leak.

Steaming mug in hand, he walked out of his office, down the long narrow corridor and into the duty sergeant's office. "Where the fuck is that DCI?" he said by way of greeting. "There's been shots fired for heaven's sake and we don't know if we have a body yet, so chase them up now."

"Yes sir, right away, I'll get on the phone now," said the Sergeant as he fumbled for the receiver. When he finished the call, he looked up at the Super. "He's seven minutes away, sir."

"He bloody well better be."

Anxiety rising, Superintendent O'Shea returned to his office, where he paced back and forth in front of his desk until, eight minutes later, a tall, well-built middle-aged man walked in

"Sorry I took so long, Sir. The traffic was a nightmare even with the blues and twos on."

The Super harumphed and moved behind his desk. "Are you fully up to speed on what's going on?"

"I think so sir, there's been a hostage situation in the library, two armed men, and shots fired just a few minutes ago, not sure if we have casualties and we think there's a leak on the team."

"Yes, that's pretty much the gist of it, unfortunately. Get to the scene and see what you can find out and keep radio chat to an absolute minimum."

The DCI strode briskly through the building, out into the yard and into his unmarked Audi A6. As he was pulling out of the station in Naas, he switched on the sirens once more and accelerated hard, tyres squealing briefly until they found some grip. He got to the old Newbridge Road and had a clear run, so he put his foot to the floor, arriving at the scene in eight minutes.

When he reached the library, he left the car on the road and jumped out, grabbing his navy Garda jacket and his Garda-issued handgun. Suited and booted, he quickly made his way down to Darcy and the firearms team.

"DCI Barry," he offered his hand. "Darcy, I don't want there to be any friction between us, this wasn't my decision."

"You have a job to do and so do I," Darcy replied gruffly. "Let's get them done."

Chapter 33

There was a surreal silence, as though the world held its breath, waiting to see what had happened. JJ felt like time has slowed to a crawl. At a snail's pace he watched the butt of the gun strike the medic's neck, then his body collapsed on the tiled floor. He heard the crack of the gun, saw the flash from the muzzle, witnessed Larry's head reeling from the kickback. All in silent, slow motion, the sound drawn out in yawning chasms, even his own voice.

"What the fuck," JJ screamed, only his scream came out as a stage whisper. Robbing a bookies was one thing, but this was a whole other ballgame and one he wasn't interested in playing. He had never considered shooting anyone. Not on this job. Not ever. This job was supposed to be easy pickings. Rob the bookies, over the bridge, straight out of town, onto the motorway, gone. Instead, here he was, under siege in a fucking library of all places with Larry of all people.

JJ could admit he wasn't exactly a criminal mastermind, was actually quite shocked when The Carpenter picked him out for this job. And what had he got himself involved in? He stared at the prostrate body on the floor and stepped over him. This medic was of no use to them.

JJ opened the door to the main library. The hostages were lined up in front of the reception area, cowering, hands over their ears. Larry was right. Three were missing. Maxwell was sitting on a chair beside Betty, a pained expression on his face.

"What have you done?" Maxwell shouted.

"Mind your business, or you'll be next." JJ shook his fist at the old man, forcing the feeling of fear back down. "Shut it, all of you."

Visibly shaking, Maxwell tried to stand but JJ strode over and pushed him back down. The librarian sat practically glued to the floor, visibly shaking and whimpering. Afraid of him. Afraid of what he might do.

Out of nowhere, JJ felt like laughing. He was in too deep now, thanks to Larry. He figured he might as well enjoy it. It was like a rollercoaster. Fear eats your insides, adrenalin hits and suddenly you're no longer scared. Instead, you're having the time of your life. The realisation suddenly hit that, for perhaps the first time in his life, he was the one with the power. These people were afraid of him. Little old JJ. The lad that failed as a boxer; who couldn't hold down a job; whose tiny brain was addled with the drugs. Whose family was ashamed of what he'd become. Ha! That was all in the past. Right here, right now, JJ was in charge. He bent down, took Betty's chin and raised her face to his.

"Do as you are told, and you won't get hurt," he spoke directly into her terrified eyes, "Or you will regret it. Do you understand me?"

She nodded and he dropped her chin, watching for a few moments as she whimpered, her eyes fixed firmly on the ground. JJ laughed aloud, relishing the idea that she was too afraid to even look at him. Behind him, the door opened, and he turned to catch a glimpse of the medic on the ground as the door closed once more after Larry. The noise levels outside had risen with sirens blaring, lights flashing and the undertone of close circuit radios. From somewhere in the sky came the whirring of helicopters. More than one. Hovering over the premises, lighting up the exterior like something out of a film set.

The phone rang. Larry and JJ exchanged glances.

"Let it ring," Larry said.

The ringing stopped after ten seconds, then rang again and again until its constant shrill sound became part of the cacophony of noise surrounding them. Larry finally marched over to the counter and picked up the receiver.

"What?" he demanded.

"It's DCI Darcy," came the voice from the other line. "We heard a gunshot. Is someone hurt?"

"No, the gun went off accidentally," Larry grunted. "It was loaded with blanks. But don't go getting any funny ideas," he quickly added. "We have magazines filled with the real thing."

"Okay, I'm glad to hear that nobody's hurt."

"Not yet, unless you go back on our deal," Larry replied, then hung up and beckoned JJ over.

"That was the guards, wondering if we'd shot anyone. Where are the three missing women?"

"I don't know. The young one, Sadie, and the older woman, Olive and the quieter one, Siobhan. I haven't seen them since we pulled that lad back inside."

He gestured towards Daniel who remained in the same position just inside the door. JJ grabbed him by the shoulders and dragged him over in front of Maxwell. Daniel moaned softly and his eyes flickered. JJ noticed the look of disdain on the old man's face as he stared down at the prostrate Daniel.

"What, you think he's an idiot too, do you?" JJ jeered.

Maxwell glanced up, a look of pure hatred flashing across his face. JJ laughed, then stepped closer to Maxwell, leaning in.

"You'd love to have a pop at me, wouldn't ye. Ye mad ole fucker," he whispered in his ear. "Go on, try me. Give me an excuse."

He cackled again as Maxwell squirmed in his seat then stood and nodded at Larry who grimaced as the phone rang yet again. JJ glanced around the library and reckoned it was time to track down Sadie. That one thought she knew all about him. She thought she could get him on side, mentioning her brother. He was surprised she remembered him, as back then she didn't pay him a blind bit of attention. JJ recognised her the minute they burst through the doors. She was older now but every bit as sexy. Sadie obviously didn't even notice that he used to follow her around like a lovesick puppy. Of course, back then he was a good boy. Focused on his boxing, on getting fit and staying fit. Sadie was more interested in older boys. Men really. With jobs and money who could treat her the way she deserved to be treated. JJ was only a lad. He wasn't even a glitch on her radar. She would pay attention to him now.

Pushing against the fire door, he stepped through and found himself in a dark corridor. There were no windows or doors, no shafts of light other than the light behind him through the open fire door. The corridor must go somewhere, he thought to himself. There's a fire door into it for a reason. JJ cocked his ear, listening for any sound but could hear nothing other than the pandemonium outside. He flicked on the flashlight on his phone and stepped forward. The corridor measured fifty paces long but went nowhere.

Puzzled, he stepped back into the hallway. He ran through the events of the past hour in his head. When Sadie and Olive called for help to drag Daniel back in, Larry volunteered him. He had pulled Daniel by the shoulders back inside the door and into the main library. He was sure Sadie and Olive were beside him. They couldn't have gone through that fire door because if they had they would still be there, hiding out in that dark hallway. So, they must have gone into the main library with him and slipped into the corridor behind the reception.

"There's nowhere out that way to hide," JJ told Larry when he returned. "They must have slipped back here."

He produced the knife and moved theatrically across the floor to the corridor behind the reception area.

"Come out, come out, wherever you are," his sing-song tone more threat than request, "Enough of your hide and seek. Here comes JJ."

Chapter 34

In The Carpenter's experience, there was a real skill in finding exactly the right screw to turn and the precise amount of pressure to apply to get someone to do exactly what you wanted them to. He always felt a deep sense of satisfaction in rooting out someone's weak spot and watching them squirm as they balanced the cost of working for a criminal against having the consequences of their actions finally catch up with them.

A politician with a hidden drinking problem, drowning in debt. A businessman fiddling his tax returns. A GAA star who bought cocaine by the kilo. Or a garda with a thirst for gambling and a penchant for young prostitutes.

The latter, he mused as he sat at the kitchen island, one hand clamped around a mug of coffee, had proven particularly useful, beyond what he could have imagined. Six years had passed since that Garda had grudgingly agreed to provide information to The Carpenter and his gang, in return for enough money to settle his debts and sate his desires. Mutually beneficial information was exchanged – forewarning of a planned raid on a warehouse full of heroin, for example, or information that led to the arrest of The Carpenter's closest rivals. And in those six years, the gang leader had risen to the top of the food chain.

Even now, posted to a quiet town in Kildare, his uniformed informant was still proving quite useful, if a little more unwilling to be his eyes and ears inside the force. But after today, it wouldn't matter. After today, if everything went to plan, nothing would matter any longer. Freedom beckoned, freedom from the glances over his shoulder, the worry of a familiar face in a crowd, steel doors all around the house, wondering who to trust.

The Carpenter picked up his phone, pressed several buttons and held it to his ear. After several rings, the other side picked up with a grunt and a short "what now?" He raised an eyebrow.

"I think you're forgetting who you're talking to," he said. His tone was even, but there was a hint of steel in the words. "Care to try that again?"

There was silence on the other end of the line for a moment, then a cough, and a muttered, "Yeah, sorry. Hello. What's up?"

"Things are about to move from our end. That window needs to stay open, as long as possible. Have you got a handle on it?"

Silence reigned again for a few moments, then there was a grunt. "I have, but I don't know for how much longer. They're talking about going in already, you know? I'm trying to keep it calm, keep us outside and them inside. But I don't call the shots here, you know that."

The steel in The Carpenter's tone sharpened and he gripped the phone tighter.

"I don't care how you do it, keep that window open," he hissed. "Two hours max, that's all I need. Find a way to keep your lot outside for that long. I don't need to tell you what happens if you don't."

"Yeah," said the voice from the other side. There was a tremor in it now. "But maybe you can have a word with those lads in the library. They're not making things easy, y'know? We've had a paramedic in there already for one of the hostages. If they keep on like that, if anybody else gets hurt, someone'll decide to go in and end it."

"They've already been warned," The Carpenter replied. "You keep your end of the deal, and we'll all make it out of this in one piece."

Chapter 35

Shock clamped Sadie's throat tight in shock. The embarrassing sob that she had felt overcoming her turned into a humiliating squeak as Olive's hand closed over her mouth. Who was this Olive that launched herself on top of Sadie? Where was the quite reserved Olive that wrote picturesque memories in the writing group? She had turned into a different person since JJ and the other guy appeared in the library and it scared Sadie nearly as much as JJ's transformation did.

With panic raising, Sadie looked into Olive's steely eyes and tried to ask what she was doing but could only manage a mumble. Keeping Sadie pinned and her hand firmly in place on Sadie's face, Olive shushed Sadie.

The slight cock to Olive's head relaxed Sadie somewhat. Olive was listening for something rather than trying to cut off her breathing. Sadie tried to settle and listen too, but the only sound she could hear was the rush of her own breathing. Olive's light but firm weight stopped Sadie from getting a full breath of air to try and calm herself and Sadie's panic started to raise again. If only she could get an arm under herself to push Olive off, she could get a deep breath. The way she had fallen over meant her arms were caught underneath her own body, and she didn't have the strength to lift herself and Olive by her stomach muscles alone. The feeling of Olive's strong fingers so close to her nose only combined to push her panic higher and she could hear and feel the frantic beating of her heart.

In desperation, Sadie shifted her weight and tried to wriggle out from beneath Olive. This small movement snapped Olive's attention back to her. In the millisecond it took for her to take in Sadie's face, Olive's eyes softened, and she shifted off Sadie.

"Sorry dear, I thought you were going to cry out and there might be people in the hall. I am going to remove my hand now, okay? Please, don't make a sound, don't move. I'm not going to hurt you."

With the pressure lifted, Sadie lay on the floor for a moment to gather herself and get her breath back. What was going on? Writing was her therapy; she did these sessions with the group to decompress and share her troubles in a semi-anonymous fashion through her made-up characters. How did she end up as a character some Hollywood hostage story? She had chosen to live in sleepy ol' Ireland, write her fiction and live her little life's dramas rather than travel the big bad world and be scared shitless in China, Africa or the Americas. Then bam! Before she knew what was happening, a nice little writing session turned into a hostage situation where poor old Maxwell has been hurt, not to mention whatever was wrong with Daniel. Olive had turned into some super spy who for a moment seemed like she was trying to kill her and who knows what JJ had done to the others by now. JJ... what had happened to him? She hadn't seen him for years, but he wasn't the same boy she had gone to school with and that had hung out with her brother. Something had happened in his life to turn him cruel and unfeeling.

As she lay on the ground, Sadie became aware that a tear was rolling down her face and that Olive was staring at her. She slowly sat up and wiped it away, but the tears started flowing faster.

"I know it's tough love, but hang in there, we will make it through this," Olive whispered, flashing her a thin smile.

"It's not that," Sadie muttered through sobs. "He died, you know?"

"Daniel didn't die, he was unconscious last time I saw him and surely will be in pain when he wakes, but he's very much alive."

"No, not Daniel," Sadie managed through the tears which created streaky tracks down her make-up. Olive took Sadie's hands in hers. "Take a breath and tell me all," said Olive.

"My dog," Sadie blurted out. "My little John-Joe died this morning."

"You poor pet, what happened?"

"Old age, I knew it was coming. I thought I was prepared. But it just hit me so hard. I shouldn't have come today; I should have stayed at home."

"I'm sorry dear, I knew you had a dog, but you never talked about him much. It's a tough blow to lose a loved one like that."

Sadie nodded. "Me and my little John-Joe were a family, strange as all as it sounds, but JJ meant the world to me and got me through some hard times when I first started living on my own."

As she talked, Sadie's breathing relaxed, tears still flowed freely but she was able to get her words out. She even noticed the slight raise of Olive's eyebrow at the abbreviation of John-Joe to JJ.

"Yes, my little angel had the same name as that brute out there," Sadie said, and before she could stop herself words were flowing out of her, and she shared the story she had always kept close to her heart.

Sadie told Olive of her history with JJ before he was the brute that had turned up that day. She explained how he had been friends with her brother, and she had had a crush on him when she was younger, though she'd always hidden it, afraid of rejection. So, when she moved out on her own for the first time and got her dog for company, she named him JJ.

"I am sorry for your loss, Sadie, he sounds like a wonderful little dog, and you will have some great memories to cherish I am sure," Olive said, patting her hand.

Sadie gave her a weak smile. Her tears had stopped for now and she did feel better having shared her grief, even if she wasn't sure if she knew the real Olive at all. Then a thought struck Sadie as the reality of her situation closed in on her again.

"Do you feel that?" Sadie asked.

"Feel what?"

"I think I feel a slight draft on my legs, is there something under the carpet?"

Olive placed her hands on the carpet near Sadie's outstretched legs and nodded her head.

"Well done girl, it does feel like a draft, there might be a trap door."

"But how do we get to it? This carpet is down tight, we'll never get it up."

"I might have something in my bag that will help," said Olive and after rummaging her hand around in her bag pulled out what appeared to be a shiny blank rectangle about one and a half fingers long. Holding the rectangle in one hand, Olive did an elaborate flick of her wrist that was accompanied by some clicking sounds.

"That's a knife! Why do you have a knife?" asked Sadie, "I don't mean to be rude, but you aren't exactly the stereotypical knife carrier."

"Don't judge a book by its cover," Olive responded with a chuckle. "But you are right, I am not a typical knife carrier, this is just a memento from my wilder days in my youth."

Without further discussion, Olive got to work trying to prise loose the edge of the carpet. Sadie watched on and again could not help but think – *who is this Olive?*

Chapter 36

Fear ate into Siobhan. Her hands trembled as her mind raced through multiple scenarios of JJ not only finding her but using that knife to make her pay for her disobedience. Her eyes darted around her hiding place. The label on a storage box directly in front of her attracted her attention. Why would birth records be stored in a library, she wondered. She vaguely remembered reading an article in the *Kildare Nationalist* about records from the county home in Athy, stored in the library. The former workhouse, converted to a mother and baby home, had a reputation. Her mother always attributed her father's propensity for violence to his early years in the county home, though Siobhan doubted that was sufficient explanation for his violent behaviour. It was an easy excuse for him. Blaming his childhood as if he had no control over his anger.

She lifted the lid, removed a thick manilla file and flicked through the contents. It struck her as sad that someone's life had been recorded in neat script, giving only the facts and no clue as to the tragedy behind the words. The language sounded archaic in this day and age. Spinster, bachelor, were those terms even used anymore? She didn't think so. Then, she noted the date at the top of the page, 1990. This was much more recent than she could possibly have imagined. Siobhan looked through the entries with increased incredulity.

March 13, 1990. Margaret McMahon, Mother's name, Mary McMahon,

April 15, 1990. Seamus Monaghan, Mother, Alice Monaghan

May 16, 1990. Angela Smith, Mother, Brigid Smith.

June 19. 1990. Martina Murphy, Mother, Maria Murphy.

Sept 18. 1990. Lawrence Costello, Mother, Elizabeth Costello

The entire column for father's name and occupation were blank, a single line drawn through them. Siobhan shook her head. So many children who had and have no idea who their father was. As a child she had often wished ill of her father, but she also wondered what it would be like to have none. Would she have been better off without him? Not so long ago those children would have been classed as bastards, illegitimate children with no rights and looked down upon by society. Thankfully times had changed, she thought, or at least she hoped so.

"Well, well, well, what have we here?"

Siobhan froze as JJ's sing-song voice sounded above her. She looked up at JJ's face peering through the shelves, a malicious glint in his eyes.

"Get the fuck out now," he hissed.

Siobhan scrambled to her feet, clutching the file to her chest, as boxes tumbled around her, their contents scattering across the floor. She felt her collar choking her as JJ roughly grabbed her and dragged her out from her hiding place.

"Get up, get the fuck back to the others."

Siobhan recoiled from the spittle out of JJ's mouth, crying out in fear and pain,

"I've had enough of this shit, do you hear me," JJ roared, and with his free hand poked the blade of his knife into the small of her back. "Now walk," he screamed in her ear.

Siobhan felt as if the walk back to the main library area took hours instead of minutes. Every inch of her body shook uncontrollably, though it was a relief to see Daniel in one piece even if he appeared to be floating in and out of consciousness and looked to be in a lot of pain. JJ nudged the knife against her back. "Sit." She whimpered as she fell into place between Betty and Maxwell, still grasping the file to her chest.

Over by the door, the medic suddenly moved, groaning as he attempted to sit up.

Larry and JJ locked eyes and JJ laughed. "I thought you killed him, man. I thought the fucker was dead"

"JJ," Larry spoke quietly, "we're still missing two women. The young one in the pink and the older, slim one with the attitude. Find them, now."

"No problem, Larry," JJ said with a confident grin. "Leave it to me."

Siobhan swallowed as JJ danced out of the room, like a boxer dancing his way out of the ring after a victorious fight. Beside her, Daniel groaned again, his complexion deathly white against his dark hair. The medic pulled himself to his knees, glanced around the library, then looked up at Larry.

"There was no need to hit me. I'm here to help the injured. I've no weapons, nothing." He shook his head and arced his back, producing an audible crack. "Where's my bag?"

"Here," Larry said, handing him the clear plastic bag.

The medic moved over to Daniel and within minutes his ankle was strapped up. He rooted around in his bag, produced a small vial and a needle, then gave Daniel an injection. After a few moments, Daniel's eyes fluttered open and looked a lot less dazed.

The medic moved on to Maxwell. His professional manner and easy assured confidence made Siobhan feel more at ease. Surely no harm would come to them with this man on their side.

"Your nose is broken," he said as he finished cleaning Maxwell's face then went to check his blood pressure. "You'll have the face of a boxer when this is all over."

"Help us, please. Larry seems a little normal," Maxwell whispered as he nodded towards their captor, "but the other guy is a nutcase. Heaven knows what he'll do to us with enough time."

"The guards have this place surrounded," the medic muttered while he pretended to search his bag for something. "Armed guards, helicopters, the lot. I don't reckon you'll have much longer to wait."

"What are you mumbling about?" Larry towered over the two men.

"I'm just checking their injuries, mate. Take it easy. I need to get them out of here."

"Not happening." Larry's tone was decisive.

"Listen, mate. The younger guy is out of it. I've given him something for the pain, but he may have a concussion. And the older guy, look at the colour of him. His blood pressure is through the roof."

"No one leaves. Not until I do. You get back outside, and you tell the guards I asked for safe passage out of here. The clock is ticking."

The medic stood but didn't make any move to leave. "It'll go in your favour if you let the injured go," he said calmly. "Let them see you don't mean to hurt anyone."

Siobhan was paralysed by fear as Larry gestured towards them with the gun.

"Not happening. You can tie this lot up before you go. Hands in their laps, where I can see them".

The medic stared at Larry, then at the gun. "Is this really necessary?" he asked.

"Yes, it is. Do it now, or you'll be joining them."

Daniel was first. The medic tied his hands loosely before giving Daniel a final check over. He moved on to Betty, who appeared to have accepted her fate. She never took her eyes off Larry.

Keep cool," the medic said as he took the file from Siobhan's hands and placed it on the ground beside her. "You'll be out of here before you know it. Just do what they say."

When he finished with Maxwell, the medic stood, flashed them a smile, then turned and faced Larry. A wave of despair washed over Siobhan as she watched Larry escort the medic to the door.

Chapter 37

Betty had felt a headache coming on for quite some time, but now as she became more anxious, it had turned into a migraine, a one-sided throbbing invading her forehead. Her heart was pounding in her chest, and her palms were sweaty.

"When will this hell be over and where is Jack and the gardai. Why haven't they come to get us out." Betty muttered as a wave of nausea washed over her. She glanced at Siobhan who smiled at her. It was a small comfort to the friends knowing that the other was okay.

As Betty let her mind drift back to her and Siobhan's first meeting, she could feel her pounding heart become a little calmer. Fifteen years had passed since they met in the library. Siobhan had been a weekly attendee on Saturday mornings, when she returned the previous week's books and browsed for more. She would often stay as long as two hours, lost in the peaceful ambiance of the library. One frosty winter Saturday, Siobhan being the only visitor in the library, Betty invited her for a coffee at the reception desk. It was then their friendship began.

"Are you okay, did he hurt you?" Betty asked her friend.

"I'm fine thanks, how are you? Your face is a bit flushed."

"A migraine, that's all, as well as being scared to flipping death. What if we don't make it out of this alive?"

Siobhan gave Betty a gentle shoulder to shoulder nudge in an attempt to reassure her. "Try not to worry. I'm sure it will be over as soon as the gardai give them what they want. You never hear of these things going south, not in Ireland. They always get resolved."

Betty nodded, but the words did little to assuage her fear and her guilt. Guilt that her friend was caught up in this horrific situation – after all, it was she who introduced Siobhan to the creative writing group. Betty remembered that first morning when, over coffee, Siobhan asked her opinion on a short story she had written, before sharing it with the group. Admiration was Betty's first feeling, wishing she had the confidence to share her own writings.

"You should get the words on paper," Siobhan had encouraged her.

"I could never let anyone read it." Betty had whispered with a smile.

Siobhan's response was gentle and considerate. "It would be good therapy and a way of dealing with your past. You know, writing my memoir under the guise of fiction and getting the members' feedback has made for some great discussions, as well as being great therapy for me in dealing with the abuse."

Based on that conversation with Siobhan, Betty had begun writing her own memoir. She carried a pen and paper everywhere. A sound, a smell, a song, any one of these often jogged a memory from her past, some good and some not so good. The more Betty wrote, the more she wanted to write. She often found herself watching the large library clock tick away the last minutes of her working day, then rushing home to expand on her notes in a word document.

Betty felt helpless being trapped and wondered, if her captors didn't get what they wanted, would she make it out of the library alive. Perhaps this was her last chance to let Siobhan know how much she valued her friendship through her writings. Betty had discreetly taken the folded sheets of her writing from her bag before they had been tied up, and as she slipped them to Siobhan, she gave a smile saying; "My memoirs, if you fancy something to take your mind off things. By the way you're mentioned, not by your real name though."

Siobhan returned the smile and began to read the first page.

'There she goes again, raising her voice to my father, what the hell – will she ever let up? Today is my sixteenth birthday and she must take the good out of it. Poor Dad, he brought home a chocolate cake instead of HER favourite, vanilla. I remember at breakfast she told him to pick up a cake on his way home from work, she didn't specify a flavour. As it was MY birthday, dad picked up MY favourite, chocolate. All the better as chocolate is my dad's favourite too. Serves the bitch right. But poor Dad. I don't remember how old I was when I first realized my mother controlled him with her bullying tactics. But as the years have gone by, I can put my hand on my heart and honestly say I detest my mother. I can feel resentment building and I know I will never be able to feel love for her. Am I a bad

daughter? Never mind, I'll answer that... after all this is my journal, and I can write what I like. No, I'm not a bad daughter, just a daughter with a bad mother. Thank God for Dad. I love him so much and wish I could make mother love him too. Then she wouldn't be so cruel to him.'

Siobhan turned a few pages and another paragraph jumped out at her.

'My poor Dad was buried today. Dear God, I miss him so much, how will I cope with her... the bitch. There she was standing over his coffin, dressed in black, and that awful creepy witch-like mantilla covering her face. For fear anyone would think she was not crying under the black lace, she gave a sob every now and then. I couldn't help feeling what a phoney she was. It was then I learned to hate black mantillas – and what was an Irish woman doing wearing a traditional Spanish lace veil? She was holding a red rose in one of her black gloved hands and a dry tissue in the other. I almost giggled at one point. Visualising my mother in Spanish dress wearing her black mantilla with the high comb called a peineta. Worn to make Spanish dancers more majestic and festive. Although Irish women did not wear the high comb, it was funny to visualise my mother attempting a Spanish dance. Thank God my poor dad can't see her faking tears.'

Chapter 38

As Siobhan read Betty's thoughts on paper, familiar feelings of upset and anguish flooded her veins, the past abuse at the hands of her husband and the abuse she witnessed her father inflict on her mother all came rushing back. The horror of what she and her mother lived through had left emotional scars.

Betty's writings were as though she was describing how Siobhan's past made her feel. Neither woman felt worthy of happiness, they lived their lives coasting from day to day. Not knowing how to be truly happy, or if they deserved to be. Always wary of others, unable to trust or be dependent on anyone. Keeping to themselves for fear and shame their past may be unveiled. The women shared feelings of daily repenting for whatever part they played in the abuses and losses in their past.

Siobhan remembered her first meeting with Betty in the library so many years ago, which led Betty to introduce Siobhan to the creative writing group, which held weekly meetings in the back room. Siobhan enjoyed her teaching job at the girls' secondary school, but she had never let her guard down enough to make friends with her colleagues. Betty was her one true friend and Siobhan looked forward to Saturday morning visits in the library with Betty before the writers' group met.

The women had so much in common. They talked about their counselling sessions, the numerous self-help books on how to deal with and ease the emotional baggage they carried from their past.

Forgiving themselves was proving to be the hardest exercise yet. Betty had taken Siobhan's advice and began writing her memoirs.

As Siobhan read the first page of Betty's memoir, she was pleasantly surprised with her writing. She felt Betty could be an excellent writer and a valued member of the writers' group, but she also knew why Betty hadn't become a member, at least not yet. Siobhan looked back at the pages and continued to read.

Losing my wonderful Dad had been the worst day of my life until today. I have been so ill these past weeks, today was the final straw and I went to the doctor. I have mixed emotions; I'm scared, I'm excited and I'm petrified of my mother. I know Jack is far from thrilled, but I also know he loves me and together we will decide the best future for our unborn baby. Being pregnant and unmarried in the 80s will not be easy. The stigma around illegitimacy for many people, including my entitled, self-centred mother, will be too much for Jack, our baby and me to bear. The do-gooders and so-called pillars of society will frown on us who find themselves in the 'family way'. They will use words like 'sinful', 'shameful', 'embarrassing to our families'. Jack and I are so young, we have second level education but still depend on our parents for our home and stability. Now that dad is gone, my mother will throw me out. No doubt she will tell her friends I have moved out of the country to a university in England or America. Anything to save face.

Jack and I are spending many hours discussing our options. What if we leave our families and got jobs, would we survive and give our baby the best start in life? However, the fear of being totally alone with no support from family will not be a good start for our baby. We have planned to see a priest from another parish next week. Hopefully he will give us guidance in making the best decision. I'm praying to God for guidance too.

Siobhan shook her head, wondering how hard it must have been for them, then turned the page and read on.

It's been three weeks since I last wrote. Two weeks ago, we went to see Fr John from Carlow. He is in his early 40s and was very understanding and made Jack and I feel welcome. He gave us advice on our options, and we are considering them before our meeting with him next week. The thought of giving our baby to a married couple to raise seems the best option. Adoption, and all its consequences for Jack and me, seems daunting, but we are both thinking it may be the best option for our baby. We want him or her to have a better start in life. Better than the start we could provide.

Siobhan suddenly thought of the file she had found just a short time ago. She thought of the names on the list of mothers, wondered if they had gone through the same anguish, deciding whether to keep their baby and endure the consequences that came with that, or give it up in the hope the little one would have a better life.

Today I felt my baby moving. It made me cry as I believe Jack is leaning towards adoption. So far, I have hidden my situation from my mother, but for how much longer? I stay out of her way as much as possible. Father John has come up with a plan which hopefully will be plausible, non-suspicious and acceptable to my mother. A farming family on the border of Kildare and Carlow have been meeting with him in the hope of adopting a child. This couple have no children of their own and desperately want a family. Fr. John can arrange for me to go to a mother and baby home in Carlow until our baby is born and he will then arrange the adoption. I will have to lie to my mother and tell her I'm taking a summer job away from home for the last two months of my pregnancy.

Jack and I are giving it a lot of consideration. My heart breaks at the thought of not seeing my child grow up, however, this is not the time to be selfish. If only my dear father were still alive, I know he would be my protector. He would encourage my relationship with Jack and us keeping our baby. As for my mother, I do believe Dad would stand up to her controlling ways and choose me, Jack, and our baby over my mother's insensitivity. I can't help wondering what will become of Jack and I after the adoption. Only time will tell.

Siobhan couldn't stop reading such a fascinating insight into her friend's past and wondered where Betty had found the strength to struggle through those days.

I miss my wonderful Dad; it's only been three months since we buried him, and my mother has moved on with her social life like he never existed. She plays bridge now at the local centre, one evening a week. She even has the nerve to go to the parish dances. I wish my *lovely Dad was here so I could talk to him, I know he would support me and give the best advice. Jack and I talked for ages last night, we have explored all possibilities and there is no way either of us can raise our baby. I'm only 18 and Jack is 19, and we know my mother will kick me out of the house if we tell her. Support and understanding in this situation would be non-existent. What the neighbours would think and the shame myself and Jack being unmarried would bring upon her would be the last straw.*

But this is not about her. It's about our baby and how Jack and I can do the best for our unborn child. Tonight, we decided adoption was the only real option. There is one thing worse than my mother kicking me out of the house, and that's me being homeless with an infant. Unfortunately for us, Jack's parents are not around to advise or help. His Dad died in a work accident when Jack was ten years old and just two years later his poor mother died of cancer. Jack believes the cancer was brought on by her broken heart after she lost the love of her life. Jack was raised by his paternal aunt. She and her husband had four children and although their children were older than Jack, his aunt and uncle didn't give it a second thought. They took Jack in and treated him like one of their own and he was grateful for their love and kindness. He knows his aunt and uncle would support us both, but he couldn't expect them to support our baby too. Once we decided to give our baby up for adoption, Jack thought long and hard about telling his aunt and uncle, but on further reflection he was afraid they would blame themselves for not raising him right.

I'm so torn about our decision. However, I know it's what's best for our child and Jack agrees with me. Dear God, please find a good home for our baby and give me and Jack peace of mind with our decision.'

Even such a short glimpse into Betty's past gave Siobhan more understanding and empathy for her friend and all she went through. She was beginning to understand why Betty was so guarded all these years. The decision she and Jack made, although the right one at the time, broke both their hearts.

As Siobhan read on, she soon discovered that the second painful heartbreak for the couple was their decision to go their separate ways, just months after the adoption was finalised. Jack joined the seminary and although they didn't meet in person, they wrote each other weekly. Neither ever mentioned their son for fear of upsetting the other. They had great respect and love, but their religion and fear of negative judgement from society – not to mention Betty's mother – played a huge part in their silence. They decided to be apart and never speak of their feelings again.

When Jack was in his final year, he decided to take his vows and do God's work. Betty decided to remain single, live at home and help care for her aging mother. They believed the celibate lives they chose would go part way to atone for their past sin.

A tear rolled down Siobhan's cheek as she read Jack's last letter to Betty, to say goodbye. He was being ordained the following week and would be sent to teach in a mission parish in Zambia. The letters were no more. They both got on with life alone, holding in their hearts the regret of giving up their son, one lonely day at a time.

Chapter 39

DCI Barry stood back on the outer cordon, watching Darcy and his cohorts. He found it hard to believe there was a mole in this outfit. They seemed so tight, so professional. Darcy's reputation in particular reputation preceded him. He was highly thought of and very nearly at retirement. His men respected him.

Barry shook his head. There was no way it was Darcy leaking information to the criminal underworld. They had been through recruit training in Templemore together. While they had never been friends as such, their careers would have mirrored one another. They had been posted to different parts of the country but enjoyed a similar rise through the ranks. DCI Barry had spent most of his career in the city, while Darcy had stayed in the country. Newbridge should be his last spot before retirement.

Barry knew it was bad practice to discount someone just because it was hard to believe, but he felt it was highly unlikely that DCI Ciaran Darcy was an informant. So, who did that leave, he wondered. He surveyed the group in front of him. Sergeant Tom Moore was deep in conversation with Darcy. Sergeant Daly, the firearms commander, was giving a briefing to his team. Barry didn't know much about either of them other than what he had read in the files before his abrupt secondment to Newbridge. They both appeared to be sound, enthusiastic and dedicated men.

Barry thought back to the specialist training. It had been drilled into them. The biggest problem in trying to find an informant is that it could be anyone. No one knows what's going on in another person's life, no matter how much of an open book they may appear to be. If anything, it's often the one person you least suspect.

Chapter 40

Larry shoved the medic out the door and slammed it shut behind him. He stood still for a minute, silently willing his heart rate to go back to normal. He couldn't take much more of this. That eejit JJ was still looking for the two women. Jeez, how long could it take to track down two women in a building this small, he thought, although that gobshite didn't have the sense he was born with. Battered out of him with every punch.

He pulled his phone from his pocket and sighed. More missed calls from Marie. The baby wasn't due for another two weeks, so that couldn't be why she needed to speak to him so urgently. It couldn't be. Larry didn't even notice his surroundings as he read through her texts, each one more urgent than the last.

"Is there something wrong?"

Larry started, almost dropping the phone. It was the librarian. Betty? He looked closer at her.

"Mind your business, Betty," he said as he put the phone back in his pocket, resolving to ring Marie later. Hopefully this fiasco would end soon. The Carpenter had promised him, two hours, no more, and they'd be extracted. He had lied about that. The two hours were nearly up, but there was no sign of the gardai backing away.

He rubbed his face, feeling the stubble that Marie hated. The thought of her sent a wave of regret crashing through his body. He had to get out of here. Taking the phone out of his pocket again he started to text her, then changed his mind again. There was no point, not until he knew he was on his way to her.

"What's this all about, Larry," Betty asked. "Can I call you Larry?"

Larry stared at her but said nothing.

"I mean, this is a library. We have nothing here of any value. Are you waiting on instructions from someone? Is there something else going on?"

"Mind your business, Betty," Larry's voice rose slightly as his phone buzzed. Another text from Marie. 'Where are you, Larry? I need you,' it read. Larry felt a lump form in the back of his throat, and he gulped involuntarily.

"What is it, Larry? Are you okay?" Betty's voice penetrated the thick fog that clouded his consciousness as he struggled to maintain control over his emotions.

"Yes. What? My wife, we're having a baby. She's texting me but the baby's not due for another two weeks. It's probably nothing."

"Hmm. Babies don't always arrive on the day they're expected. Sometimes they choose their own time of arrival."

"Oh God, I hope not," Larry said with a shake of his head, as if the idea wasn't already haunting him. The shrill ring of the phone on the desk caught his attention. He strode behind the counter and lifted the receiver.

"Yes?"

"DCI Darcy here. Who am I speaking to?"

"Have you arranged safe passage for us yet?"

"Not yet, but…"

Larry cut off any further conversation by hanging up the phone. He leaned against the counter and swallowed. In the background, he could hear the faint sound of JJ's sing-song voice taunting the women wherever they hid, like something out of a creepy nursery rhyme. The phone rang again. Larry watched and waited until the third ring. He picked up the receiver, put it to his ear and waited.

"DCI Darcy again. Look, I'm working on it. It's taking more time than I would have liked, but you didn't help matters by using that gun."

"I already explained it was a blank. That time."

"We know that now, but at the time…"

Larry waited.

"Look, the pizzas are here. In the meantime, we'll work on getting this situation resolved, okay?"

"Leave the pizzas on the step, to the right of the door. I'll send someone out. And no funny business," he warned, then hung up the phone.

"JJ," he shouted. No answer. Larry moved to the corner of the room, closest to the corridor, keeping an eye on the hostages, and shouted again. Still no answer, only the faint sound of JJ's manic sing-song.

"For fuck's sake," he muttered. "I may get them myself."

Chapter 41

Olive made short work of the carpet and quickly had it pulled back to revel a trapdoor. For a slight woman she had a lot of hidden strength Sadie thought. The trap door was made of the same dark stained wood as the floor, but it made no attempt to hide with two large bronze hinges securely bolted on one end of the door. As another indication of economic retrofitting the trap door had a modern stainless-steel lock and sliding bolt. What little hope Sadie has been kindling of an escape snuffed out when she saw the lock.

"So that's that then," Sadie said with a groan.

"Don't be so quick to give up my dear, it might not be locked."

Olive reached out and gave the sliding bolt a good rattle, it was indeed locked.

"Can I give up now?"

Olive cast a disapproving eye on Sadie.

"I should really give you one of those talks on the youth of today giving up too easily." Olive continued with a slight grin. "But perhaps now is not the best time. Where is that key that Betty gave us."

Olive fished in her bag and quickly pull out the key. It slid easily into the lock. Sadie found that she was holding her breath as she waited for Olive to turn the key. There was a bit of life in her hope yet. Smoothly Olive turned the key and the lock clicked. With a slight squeal of protest the bolt slide open.

"You might help we with this, it's a bit heavy." Olive said as she tried to lift the door open. Sadie scrambled forward to help and felt her hope raising as the stiff hinges gave out and the door opened. Was it possible that this nightmare was going to end, and this was her way out? Was escape possible?

When the door opened fully, Sadie could see that it revealed an old but sturdy looking wooden ladder. The light pouring in from the trap door showed a room, full shelves sagging under the weight forgotten items stacked on them. It looked like a place where old boxes, books and manila folders went to die. It was impossible to determine how big the room was as no walls were visible in the rectangle of light provided from the trapdoor.

Sadie could see an old-fashioned circular light switch on a pillar near the ladder. Hoping against hope that this would hold her escape route, Sadie went down the ladder leaving Olive to follow. On reaching the floor she immediately tried the switch, flicking it down. Nothing happened. Not even the slight hum some bulbs make when warming up. Sadie tried flocking the stitch up and down again but still no light. She suddenly lost her confidence that this might be an escape route, in a maze of shelves with no light. The darkness was no longer as welcoming as it had been when she descended the ladder. Sadie turned to tell Olive maybe this wasn't such a good idea as there was no light, but her words were cut off by the bang of the trapdoor closing and the echo of the bolt locking. The darkness around Sadie was total.

Chapter 42

All eyes were trained on the library door as it opened slowly. The medic was pushed out, his hands in the air. He stumbled on the step but righted himself and moved forward to the cordon.

"This is bordering on the ridiculous," DCI Barry murmured to DCI Darcy.

Darcy shot him a look that bordered on insubordinate then made his way over to where the medic was getting dressed back into his green paramedic overalls.

"Right, Brendan, what can you tell me?"

"Fucker clocked me on the back of the head the minute I stepped inside the door," Brendan rubbed his head, "lucky he didn't kill me."

DCI Darcy waited patiently.

"Two guys. One early 20's, blocky, dirty fair hair, clean-shaven, tattoo on the back of his neck. Looked like a boxer type, I'd say steroid addict. The other one is tall, dark brown hair, athletic build, mid 30's. He's in charge. I only saw four hostages, but I heard the older guy tell the younger one to go find the two missing women. That younger lad is dangerous, either high on something or totally lost the plot."

DCI Darcy nodded as DCI Barry took notes.

"And the hostages?"

"Daniel, early 20s, fell through the roof. Slipping in and out of consciousness when I got there. He's stabilised, strapped up his ankle, don't think it's broken but definitely damaged, cuts and bruises, query concussion. Elderly man, named Maxwell, broken nose, hypertension, needs to go to hospital and soon. Woman Betty, early 50s, clearly distraught but no obvious injuries. Woman, Siobhan, early 60s, no obvious injuries."

"That's great intel. Thanks Brendan," DCI Darcy said.

DCI Barry motioned to Darcy to walk with him.

"I have an idea to flush out our mole. Just follow my lead."

DCI Darcy raised an eyebrow but said nothing.

"Sergeant Moore," Barry gestured across the cordon.

"Yes Sir."

"The situation inside is worse than we thought. All six hostages are injured, some worse than others. We need to find a way to get in there and quickly. You know the library layout. Have you any suggestions?"

Sergeant Moore looked thoughtful. "Do you know where in the library they are being held?"

"Yes, in the main room, at the reception desk."

"The only suggestion I have is one that's already been put forward. But I would be worried if we move too soon, we will make matters worse."

"Agreed," said DCI Barry, "thanks Tom. Will you check that the cordon on the Athgarvan Road is still tight. I don't want anyone slipping out that way. And can you tell Sergeant Daly I'd like a word."

"Yes, of course," Sergeant Moore glanced at DCI Darcy before heading over to Daly.

"Sergeant Daly," DCI Barry signalled to him to move closer, as if to emphasise that their conversation was for their ears only. "Two hostages have escaped. We're keeping it quiet for the moment. But just so you're aware, when the order comes, it's four hostages you're rescuing, not six."

"Great news, Sir."

"But Daly, keep that to yourself. I'll let you know when you can tell your team."

"Okay," Daly looked puzzled, "Can I ask why?"

"All in good time, Daly."

Chapter 43

Betty couldn't take her eyes off Larry, all the while thinking if her secret partner was one of the gardai out front. Remembering back two years previously.

It was a Saturday morning in July, filled with sunshine and warmth, so welcomed by the Irish. Betty woke early and remembered it was her day off. Laying still with no definite plans, other than a walk, she contemplated making plans for the afternoon. As she pulled the covers back, Rex jumped from his rug onto the bed and began to nuzzle her neck. Stroking his head, she whispered

"Hey Rex, how about our walk by the river and into the park"? The words walk and park were enough for her beloved dog and true friend to hop off the bed and wag his tail.

He was a Golden Retriever she had rescued from the pound the summer before. He loved his weekend runs in the park as much as Betty did. Getting away from her mother was such a pleasure. The older Angela Costello grew, the more demanding she became. Bettys work at the library five days a week was her refuge. However, the weekends could be consumed by her mother's demands if she let them.

Since Rex joined the family, he was Betty's reason for putting on her coat and walking out the door when she needed a break.

"Are you up yet?" her mother shouted from the other room. "Or would you like to see me die of hunger?" Her voice snapped Bettys' mind back to her first commitment of the morning. Get Angela out of bed and prepare breakfast.

When her mother was settled in her favourite spot in front of the television, Betty put Rex on the lead, and they headed for the river. A few hours away from Angela, a walk in the morning sunshine and a take-out coffee from Costa was always welcomed.

Walking past her place of work she smiled and wondered where have the last twenty-five plus years gone? She loved working in the library and had no intentions of leaving it. It was her place of peace and tranquillity. Truth be told, it was her safe place to hide from the world and her past. Neither of which she could forget nor forgive herself for.

"Hey Betty, come take a look," she heard Sally call from the door of the library. "The books have arrived," Checking the traffic each way, Betty waved at Sally and crossed the road. Sally was the Saturday librarian. A young mother of two boys, full time at home on weekdays and loved her few hours in the library on Saturday mornings, while her husband spend time with the children.

Betty led Rex behind the reception desk, gave him a bowl of water and told him to stay. She followed Sally to the back room, on opening the box she was elated by the crisp smell of the newly printed books. The blend of ink, water, solvent, and finisher was a familiar and comforting smell.

Taking an arm full of books, the girls began to stack the shelf that lay waiting for this treasure of fictional books by Female Irish Authors. 'Anybody Out There?' and 'This Charming Man' by Marian Keyes, 'Thanks for the Memories' and 'P.S. I Love You' by Cecelia Ahern, 'Devoted Ladies' and 'Good Behaviour' by Molly Keane, 'Philippa's Folly' and Philippa's Flight' by Louise Couper, 'Too Close for Comfort' and 'If I Never See You Again' by Niamh O'Connor, and the latest from local author Maria McDonald, The Keeper of Secrets.

With a smile of excitement, and an arm full of books, Betty turned the familiar corner from the storeroom and bumped full force into someone. The books crashed to the ground as Betty let out a shriek of

"Oh My God, my books," the person she bumped into said, "Hell! I'm So Sorry"

They both scurried to pick up the books which were strewn over the steps and the floor. Getting to their feet, both profusely apologising.

"Betty Costello, how the heck are you, it's me Jack." Betty looked at him in silence, for what seemed like forever, before she ventured to answer. It had been thirty-one years since they had laid eyes on each other.

That Saturday morning, Jack found himself browsing in the library. He had moved back to Kildare after his promotion to Sergeant just a few months prior. Settling into the new station, taking on new cases and setting up home had taken up most of his time. He didn't know what had happened to Betty after their split. He joined the priest hood and spent many years in different dioceses in Africa.

After leaving the priest hood, he returned to Ireland and joined the Gardai, he worked his way up the ranks to the position of Sergeant, which had been a long and arduous career.

"Betty," he said as his face lit up with that familiar smile, she remembered each night for the past thirty-one years. Her heart missed more than a beat as she said

"Jack Fitzgerald, as I live and breathe. What are you doing here"?

"Just browsing if that's ok."

The next day they met for lunch and spent hours talking about their lives since college, and their heart wrenching split after they gave up their son for adoption. Jack believed Betty had moved on and was probably married with a family. Betty believed he was still a priest working abroad.

After the chance encounter with Jack in the Library two years before the day JJ and Larry burst into the library. Betty couldn't wait to tell Siobhan. When their meetings became more frequent and serious, Siobhan was her go to friend whom she confided in.

Betty remembered the day vividly. Almost like a teenager, full of excitement she called her friend with the news. Siobhan was peeling potatoes at the kitchen sink, she set her mobile on speaker and listened intently as Betty described how she met Jack that morning in the library.

"I wasn't officially working, I popped in to look at the latest novels that were delivered. There I was, thrilled to unbox the books and see them stand proud on the shelves. We accidently bumped into each other on the steps as I came from the storeroom."

"Bumped into who, who the hell are you talking about Betty? Calm down, take a breath or you'll give yourself a stroke."

"Jack, I met Jack Fitzgerald, he's back, he left the priesthood. He's living in Kilcullen. We are having dinner tomorrow. Oh my God Siobhan did you hear me? Are you there? Has the bloody line gone dead? Flipping mobiles."

"I'm here silly, listening to every word, calm down and tell me more."

Today sitting in the library as a hostage was not where she ever imagined she would be. Remembering her many conversations with Jack over the past two years she knew his superior was DCI Darcy. She wondered and prayed that Jack had been detailed to the hostage situation in the library and was working on getting her and the writing group freed.

Chapter 44

Maxwell watched Larry move to the front door. He didn't particularly like pizza, had never understood how cheap Naples Street food became so popular in Ireland. It certainly wasn't a meal served when he was growing up. He doubted he had even heard of pizza before he married in his mid-twenties. Maybe in American films but certainly not in his house. The first time he ate pizza was when his wife bought the frozen variety for treat night for their children. A wave of nostalgia hit him, constricting his chest. The boys loved it. Friday night pizza, followed by a Cadbury's chocolate bar of their choice, in front of the telly watching an X-travision video. The longing for those simpler days settled around his shoulders like a blanket. What would he give to have those days back? If only he could turn back the clock, erase his mistakes, start all over again. He could be a better father, a better husband. A better man, his inner voice whispered.

Beside him Daniel struggled against the rope binding his hands in front of him.

"What are you doing?" Maxwell hissed, "We're in enough trouble thanks to you."

"Me," Daniel looked up wide eyed, "Take a long hard look at yourself. You thought all you had to do was order them out. Look where that got you."

"Gentlemen, please," Siobhan said. "We need to figure out how to get out of here, not bicker with one another."

"Bicker," Daniel said, "tell that old fool to stay quiet."

"Why did you have my diary? Who gave you the right to go through my briefcase? How dare you." Maxwell felt the tone of voice rise as anger bubbled up inside him.

Daniel's cheeks flamed crimson, "Yea, yea, I'm sorry, okay? I was looking for something to help us. A knife, or a phone or something useful. I don't know why I took your diary. Honestly. I didn't read it. I didn't know JJ..."

"You didn't know JJ would what? Read it out loud, my...," Maxwell felt rather than heard the start of a tremble in his voice. He swallowed then cleared his throat in the awkward silence. Strains of JJ's singsong voice carried into the room sending a shiver down Maxwell's back.

"We need to concentrate on getting out of here," Siobhan said.

"How?" Maxwell shook his hands, trussed up in front of him, "Our hands are tied, literally."

"Larry will be back any minute. So will JJ when he realises the food has arrived. Has anyone any ideas?" Siobhan's whispered plea sounded frantic to Maxwell's ears.

"You're right, my dear," he tried to sound reassuring, hoping that in putting Siobhan at ease he could settle his own inner fears. This day was proving to be more traumatic than the robbery all those years ago. He prayed he would do the right thing and not embarrass himself like he had in the past.

"JJ is a loose cannon. We have to be very careful around him," Maxwell said.

"JJ," Daniel eyebrows shot up under his hairline, "they're both fecking nut jobs. Don't forget Larry is the one with the gun."

"But is it loaded?" Betty interjected. They all turned to look at her.

"We all heard the shot," Maxwell said.

"Yes, we heard it, but he didn't shoot anyone. Firing that shot was for effect. Was it a blank?"

"Well, I'm not prepared to take that chance, Betty. Just because he hasn't shot any one yet doesn't mean he won't if he needs too." Daniel shook his head.

"But what if Betty's right? What if that gun is a fake? There's four of us. We could overpower him," Maxwell said.

"What should we do, old boy. Call him over and ask him to kneel in front of me so I can undercut his chin with a belt from these." Daniel shook his tied wrists.

"I can get to my feet from this position," Siobhan said.

"So can I," said Betty.

"Well, I bloody well can't," Daniel indicated his strapped-up ankle.

Maxwell groaned. They were going round in circles.

"I think we have a better chance with Larry than with JJ. I don't think Larry would shoot anyone. It looks to me like he's in over his head, like someone else is pulling the strings," Betty said.

"He was talking to someone on the phone. JJ didn't look to happy about it," Maxwell said.

Daniel snorted. "Sweet Jesus, you two will be telling us next that Larry is a good guy. He's the one with the gun, people. Wake up."

"I didn't say he was a good guy, Daniel. I just think he shows a certain reluctance about the whole situation. He's certainly tries to keep JJ in check," Betty's face coloured.

"Maybe, but that doesn't make him a good guy, that just makes him smart and to be honest, being smart makes him more dangerous."

Maxwell wondered if Betty had a soft spot for Larry. She certainly never took her eyes off him. Maybe a touch of Stockholm Syndrome, Maxwell thought although it's a bit early in the proceedings for that. One thing he was sure of, they couldn't just sit here waiting to be rescued. There must be something they could do.

"Daniel's right. We need to be wary of both of them," Siobhan said, "but we need to do something. JJ's becoming more

193

unpredictable and as for Larry, we don't know what he will do if the Garda don't give in to his demands."

"Whatever we do, it has to be soon, before that other nutter comes back," Maxwell tried to push himself upright but flopped back down, exhausted by the effort.

Chapter 45

Betty's journal lay on the ground between Siobhan and Betty, beside the file Siobhan had unintentionally brought clutched to her chest when JJ had found her in the storeroom. Siobhan drew Betty's attention to the white sticker on the front of the manilla folder, which read, 'BIRTHS 1989'. That's all. Siobhan looked at her friend as the blood drained from Betty's face.

"What the hell Betty, you look like you've seen a ghost!"

Good God Betty thought, this must have come from the Records section in the Library in Athy. Just a couple of weeks earlier Betty received a memo from the Athy Library, advising they were sending boxes of records for temporary storage while their storeroom was being renovated. Betty hadn't given the boxes a second thought, nor had she looked at the labels to know what records they were.

Fixated on the label of the file beside her, the year had been of major significance to Betty. It was the year that changed her life 33 years ago. A loneliness and longing ache welled in her heart as she remembered the day her beautiful baby boy was born. What followed was the agonising talks with Jack, the baby's father, and an adoption councillor.

The day came when Betty and Jack signed away their baby, leaving an emptiness and horrendous pain in their hearts. The pain lingered for years. Some days it was so severe she thought it might kill her. Remembering the many nights, she lay awake feeling the pain, praying for it to ease.

With counselling and many self-help books Betty was somewhat happy, however, meeting Jack again had brought such peace to her life and mind. Another nudge from Siobhan brought Betty's attention back to the present situation. Immediately her eyes darted from Siobhan to Larry, her mind and heart forcing her to look closer at the papers in the file.

Betty edged her tied hands forward and eased the first sheet of paper out of the manilla file. Her eyes darted from line to line and there it was,

September 18, 1989, Lawrence Costello, Mothers name, Elizabeth Costello.

Shock set in as the old familiar ache in her heart and horrendous pain in the pit of her stomach returned. Siobhan had been keeping watch on their captors as Betty scanned the file.

"Hurry up, or he'll catch you," she whispered. It took another few seconds before Betty spoke.

"It's him, It's him. I knew I recognised those striking blue eyes, his mannerisms, and look at his fingers, his unruly dark hair too. Just like his fathers

"It's who?" Siobhan continued to whisper.

"Dear God, can I be right, is…. is…. he my son, oh my God, I can't believe it," Betty sobbed.

"Jesus Betty, be quiet or you'll get us all in trouble," Siobhan said in a loud whisper.

"I'm as sure as I've ever been about anything." Betty's voice was soft and gentle as she processed the facts that were unfolding.

Chapter 46

While he put on a brave face for the benefit of the others, particularly Maxwell, Daniel was worried. Their two captors seemed to be growing increasingly unstable, and it didn't look like the gardaí were coming to their rescue any time soon. What were they doing outside? Were they planning on storming the library? And, if they did, would he and the others get caught in the crossfire?

He winced as a jolt of pain shot through his head, which had been aching ever since he fell through the roof. The pain in his ankle had subsided, thanks to whatever the medic had injected him with, but his stomach was turning, and the fluorescent lights overhead were making him feel worse. He wondered if he had concussion. He'd hit his head pretty hard on the ground.

When Larry wasn't looking, Daniel strained against the rope around his hands again, trying in vain to find a weakness. Beside him, Maxwell grunted, but didn't say anything. Daniel felt another pang of guilt over what he'd done. When he found the older man's diary in the meeting room, he'd taken it in case there was something a little embarrassing between the pages, something he could use to needle him the next time Maxwell was being insufferable towards him. He hadn't realised the type of secret Maxwell had been carrying around, the shame he'd been living with. And now, because of him, the others knew about it too.

"I'm sorry," he muttered at Maxwell, who didn't look at him.

Daniel stared at the ground. He knew all about shame, how it flooded your body, pulled you down into the depths like an anchor. Six years of non-stop bullying will do that to you. Was he any better than the bullies who made his secondary school years a living nightmare? Had he done to Maxwell what they had done to him every day, humiliating him in front of everyone?

Daniel couldn't stop his mind from slipping back to that horrific experience, as fresh as though it had been yesterday. A tsunami of thoughts returned, unbidden, of being shoved and kicked down the hallway, dragged into empty classrooms and pummelled for no reason, his locker ransacked, lunch money stolen, schoolbags ripped open and tossed into bins. The taunts and the name-calling. The belittling. He'd never understood why the others in his class had stood by and let it happen. Maybe they were relieved it wasn't them, scared that if they opened their mouths, they'd be next. Teachers knew, but never did anything. The bullies were too clever to hurt him when the teachers were around, or where there were cameras. And Daniel had never said a word about who was hurting him, terrified that it would just make things worse. Instead, he'd quietly endured six years of constant fear, putting a fake smile on his face when he came home, disappearing into the fictional worlds he created on paper, longing for the day when he could walk through the school doors and never look back.

Daniel's cheeks burned red as he thought about how he had bumped into his chief tormentor a few months back in Tesco. Peter –

taller now, and balder – but otherwise unchanged – had stared at Daniel for a few moments before breaking into a smile and asking how he was. As if he hadn't tortured Daniel for years on end, made his life a living hell. Daniel had just stared at him, wondering how someone could be so cruel and pretend like it never happened. There were a million things he'd wanted to say to Peter, to shout at him, scream. Accusations and recriminations he'd rehearsed in the shower a thousand times over the years. But he just walked away. His counsellor would have been proud.

Anger brought on by those thoughts flooded his body and Daniel tugged at the rope around his hand again, but it was no use. He shifted from side to side, trying to get more comfortable, then frowned as he suddenly realised there was something hard in his back pocket. It was small, by the feel of it, and slim and he racked his brains, wondering what it could be. A pen, perhaps? But the fountain pen he used for their writing sessions was in his backpack in the meeting room. What was it? And then he remembered finding the small red penknife in Sadie's purse and slipping it into his pocket, and the anger and worry was replaced by a sudden flash of hope and determination.

Chapter 47

The thud of heavy boxes and a sharp squeak from the darkness hurried Olive's steps. Sadie is a sweet girl but panics easily, thought Olive as she carefully descended the ladder letting touch be her guide.

"What happened Sadie, are you ok?" Olive whispered into the darkness.

"No, I don't like the dark."

The tremble in Sadie's voice was a worry. Was she going to break down again? Olive didn't have time to babysit if she was going to be any use to Darcy. Time wasn't her friend at the moment, and yet what this poor girl needed was a friend.

Olive pulled out her phone and flicked on the flashlight. The area around her lit up to show Sadie sprawled at the foot of a steel industrial shelves covered in an array of books and spilled cardboard boxes.

"Are you hurt?"

"Bruised, and something heavy fell on my knee in all this, but I think I am ok? You have your phone? How is that possible I thought they took everyone's phone?"

"You would be surprised what an innocent old woman can get away with," Olive said with a wink. "Come on let's get you up out of that."

Olive helped Sadie to her feet but when she put her weight on her injured knee to walk her leg buckled underneath her. If it wasn't for Olive's support, she would have fallen back down.

"I don't think it is broken," said Sadie. "I think it is just a dead leg, this sort of thing has happened before when the hockey ball hits me in the wrong spot on my leg. I just might need a few minutes."

Minutes I don't have thought Olive, and as if to reinforce the thought the trapdoor above them rattled hard. Olive felt Sadie physically jump beside her, and Olive nearly jumped herself when Sadie scream of fright blasted into her ear. Olive clamped her hands over her mouth in an effort to shut off the noise, as what little colour she had left drained from her face.

"Don't worry, I locked the door, "whispered Olive and give Sadie a gentle squeeze. "He can't get down here."

As if in response to this a muffled voice drifted down through the trapdoor.

"This lock won't stop me for long. I heard you down there. Enough of this hide and seek, come up now and I will be gentle."

"What do we do now," Sadie asked in obvious terror.

"Well, there is no point hanging around here. He's all talk." Olive responded forcing as much confidence into her voice as she could manage. "We should go exploring to find a way out, and hopefully I will pick up a bit of phone coverage down here."

With no idea which direction to take Olive chose the gap between the shelves on the right. They set off weaving through the maze of floor to ceiling shelves, each leaden down with forgotten words. In one hand Olive held out her phone lighting the route ahead and in the other she held on to Sadie providing what physical support she could. The going was slow and the space between the shelves was tight, but Olive felt the further right they went the damper the musty air tasted on her tongue. Where the getting closer to wall? Wall usually had doors, maybe her luck was turning.

A groan escaped Sadie's lips and her face told the story of the growing pain from her leg as they hobbled along.

"Let's rest her a minute." Olive said has she leaned Sadie up against the bookshelves.

"But we don't have time to stop." But even ask she said it Sadie slipped to the floor holding her leg and rubbing it tenderly.

Not bothering to answer Olive took the rest time to have a better look around. Direct the light beam from her phone she studied the shelves. Olive took in the dark spines of beaten books with the odd flash of gold from a title as she surveyed the chipboard shelves within the metal frames. Mixed in with the books in no discernible order were faded boxed with yellowed pealing labels. As she pivoted to inspect the shelves behind her something bright flashed back from the phone light. It appeared to be a metal pipe of some sort with short cantilever ends. Its dull shine was so out of place with everything else Olive was drawn to it. Pulling it out, it was a hollow pipe about 3 feet long and three inches in diameter with bolt holes on both cantilevered ends. It must be part of the inner construction of the shelves left behind and forgotten during their construction or during maintenance at some stage. The dusty weight left good in her hand, not too heavy but yet substantial.

A gasp from Sadie made Olive spin around to her again pipe in hand.

"I think I heard the trap door open," Sadie said in an urgent whisper. "You said he wouldn't be able to open it."

"I'll go find out, wait here."

A flash of inspiration sent adrenaline coursing through Olive, she could feel her heartbeat quicken and a tingling starting deep in her calves.

"Wait don't leave me," said Sadie almost forgetting to whisper. "Please don't leave me in the dark."

Without looking back Olive tossed the phone to Sadie and disappeared around a corner.

Chapter 48

Siobhan couldn't hear what Larry was saying to Betty, so she continued to read the heart-breaking words Betty had written as her tears began to cloud her sight.

Dear Diary, tired and all as I am I must write this entry before today is over. It's the 18th of September 1989, the weather is calmer now than it was last night. We had the mother and father of all storms. The thunder made the loudest rumbling sound I ever heard, lasting seconds before its big boom. Lightning followed, which lit up the sky with flashes of red, purple, and orange. As a deluge of rain and hail pounded my bedroom window. Besides the storm, my baby had a very active night too.

No wonder I hadn't slept. I forced myself out of bed to shower and attend for breakfast, but this was a step too far, I felt weak and dizzy, my breathing was shallow, I reached for the 'call button' and lowered myself on to the chair next to the shower. The pain in the pit of my stomach was excruciating. I doubled in two and there I lay slumped motionless and limp in the chair. The last thing I remember before I lost consciousness was my waters breaking.

When I woke, I was in an ambulance on route to the maternity hospital. At 11.55am my beautiful baby boy was born.

Dear Diary, today is 30th of October, it's been six weeks of mixed emotions since my son was born. I smile every time I see or hold my precious boy. I cry with loneliness when I'm away from him. I knew *today was coming. Signing the dreaded adoption papers and giving my son to his new family.*

Dear Diary, today is December 18th it's been a tough couple of months, and today is just one week away from Christmas Day, it's also the day I part from my son forever. How cruel life can be. My eyes are sore, swollen, and red from crying. My stomach is permanently in a knot. I don't want to give him up; however, I know it's to give my perfect little boy a better start. Dear God, please help the ache in my heart to ease.

Chapter 49

"Thank God for cable ties," Larry said, "is that better than having your hands tied with rope?"

"It's not. What would be better is if we weren't restrained at all," Maxwell said.

"Now Max, Can I call you Max? Yes, good. If you lot would just do as you're told and stay put, we wouldn't have to restrain you."

Larry opened two of the pizza boxes and placed them on the table.

"At least now you can eat."

Larry retreated to the reception desk with a large pepperoni pizza and a can of coke. Finding that pack of cable ties was a stroke of luck. Waiting on the call that the pizza had been delivered he had been racking his brain trying to figure out how he could let them eat without taking off their restrains. It was simple really. Untie Maxwell, lead him over to the table, fasten his left leg to the table leg and leave his hands free. Then Siobhan, right leg to table leg, then Daniel, then Betty. They were seated around the table as if they were at a dinner party. Pizza boxes in the middle of the table, within everyone's reach, cans of orange and bottles of water in front of them. He even gave them individual napkins and those wooden, disposable, cutlery that have become so popular.

They stopped grumbling and started eating, throwing the occasional disdainful looks in his direction. What a fuck up, he thought. The library should have been empty at that time of the evening. Taking hostages wasn't part of the plan. None of this was part of his plan. He should be with Marie right now. Taking care of her, taking care of their baby. His child, his flesh and blood. Instead, I'm locked in a bloody library with a lunatic and a bunch of scribblers. Larry wiped his hands on a napkin and reached for the can.

"Damn it," Larry said as the contents of the can spilled onto the desk. He grabbed a bunch of napkins to contain the liquid, but some spilled onto the ground. He got up and went around to mop up the floor. It was then he noticed the blue file lying on the ground where the woman had been sitting. Curious, he picked it up before settling himself back down on his chair with another slice of pizza. Something on the spine of the file caught his attention.

St Vincent's Home 1989

"What the fuck…."

He hadn't realised he uttered those words aloud, until he felt the eyes of all four hostages staring at him. Larry cleared his throat, took a bit of pizza and pulled the file closer. This was definitely worth a read. While Larry didn't have all the details about his birth mother, the one thing he did know was that he was born in St. Vincent's in Athy. He never wanted to find out any more than that. Larry always knew he was adopted. His parents never hid that from him. If anything, they encouraged him to trace his birth mother, but he reckoned that if she gave him up at birth then she must have had her reasons. His brother was different. He wanted to know, traced his birth mother but that was a disaster. It all looked good at first. She appeared to be wealthy, delighted to reunite with him but her issues soon came to the fore. Her issues became his. Look where that led him. What it did to them both.

Larry flicked through the pages. His stomach clenched when he reached September 1989. The tremble in his hand visible as it rested on the page. Larry closed his eyes, taking a deep breath. Did he really want to read it? Did he really want to know his birth mother's identity? Look at what happened to Ben. The two of them were in enough trouble without adding to it.

Yet part of him wanted to know. Especially now that Marie was pregnant with his child. There was stuff he needed to know. Medical facts for example. Hereditary illnesses. Heart disease? Cancer? Huntington's disease? He had talked about it with Marie. There was a huge hole in his history that his parents couldn't fill, no matter how much they wanted to. That missing part of himself only became apparent to him when Marie told him she was pregnant. Knowing he was about to be a father changed everything.

18th September, 1989   Child's name   Lawrence

                                  Mother's name   Elizabeth Costello

                                  Father's name   --------------------

Larry stared at the entry. He was surprised to feel elated, excited even. The woman who gave birth to him has a name. Elizabeth Costello. Costello. He liked the sound of that. Elizabeth. He wondered if she went by her full name. It sounded quite posh. Did she shorten it to Liz or Lizzie, Beth maybe? Larry wondered if he looked like her. Has he got her eyes, her colouring? What genetic makeup did he inherit from Elizabeth Costello? So many questions. Maybe it's time to find out the answers, he thought. Then it struck him.

"Why was this file here?" He lifted it in the air and gestured towards Betty, who looked puzzled.

"Sorry, that's my fault. It was in a box in the back room. I had it in my hand and brought it with me," Siobhan said. "Sorry Betty."

"The records from St Vincent's," Betty said as she stared at Larry. "They were delivered yesterday. We haven't started sorting them yet."

Recognition slowly dawned on Larry. He felt as if a fog moved up though his body lifting the veil in front of his eyes and directing him to the library name tag on Betty's right side. Betty Costello. Elizabeth. Betty. It couldn't be, could it?

Chapter 50

I have to be dreaming, thought Sadie. This has to be some weird nightmare, maybe this is a side effect to that anti-anxiety medication I just started? Sadie, however, knew it was all wishful thinking, the pain in her leg was very real, and it was the pressure in her bladder that put the last nail in the coffin of her hope that this was all a nightmare. If she were truly asleep, she would have woken up by now to use the bathroom.

The light beam around her shook, and she looked down to see it was her hands that were shaking, in fact her whole body was shaking. Was she going into shock? Was she having some sort of attack? Would JJ or that other guy come along and find her shaking on the floor unable to run away? That thought froze her and so it was a moment or two before the sounds of footsteps filtered through her eyes and into her brain.

There was no time for any thoughts of running, at the same time realisation hit Sadie, JJ came into view his phone lighting the way and a nasty looking knife in the other.

"What are you doing down here Sadie?" he asked as he continued forward menacingly, "Why are you making this hard for me.? You actually think I don't remember you; what a stuck- up cow you were."

Shuffling blade and phone into one hand, JJ reached down to grab Sadie.

"Come on back upstairs, and you better give me that phone."

As JJ's sinuous grip closed on Sadie's arm, Olive appeared like a wraith behind him. Olive's eyes appeared to sparkly and as if in slow monition. Sadie watched in awe as Olive swung the mental pipe at his head. Spots of blood exploded from where the pipe connected with JJ's skull. Bits of this blood splattered across Sadie's face as she closed her eyes, she felt his grip go slack and JJ weight fell away to the side. This was followed by a heavy crash, but Sadie didn't take much notice. All her focus and disgust were on the feeling of a large pearl of blood weaving its way down the side of her face. She was covered in blood, JJ's blood, human blood. This thought reached her stomach, and it rolled in revolt. Before she could do more the eruption of her stomach overtook her and with her eyes still closed, she rolled onto all fours and vomited. The sound of the splatter on the polished concrete floor and the feel of the spray on her bare hands and arms created a vicious cycle of eruptions. She emptied her stomach and continued to dry retch as the powerful stench tried to gag her on the few breaths she could get between bouts.

Refusing to open her eyes she scrambled backwards until her feet hit something hard and blocked her retreat. Sadie collapsed to the floor whimpering, the cool floor a small comfort on her face in her ocean of torment.

Time held no meaning for Sadie as she lay there until she felt gentle cloth rub her face and arms.

"It's the shock love. You will be alright," Olive said, "Sit up so I can clean you off."

Sadie complied and after a few moments of being rubbed down she risked opening her eyes.

Olive hoovered before her in the afterglow of the phone lights. Olive finished brushing off Sadie's clothes, she threw the cloth with badly frayed edges to the side as she stood up. A part of Sadie's mind wondered where she got the cloth but mostly, she was thankful to be somewhat clean. If she breathed through her mouth, she could almost ignore the smell.

"I need your help over here," said Olive. "I know you're in shock, but we don't have much time. Just do as I say."

Sadie nodded dumbly.

"Up on your feet so."

Sadie followed Olive over to where the shelves had fallen over like dominos and created a shallowed angle with the floor as they lay partially stacked on one another. Numbly Sadie took in the scene of JJ tied to the bottom of the first toppled shelve with blood trickling down the side of his head. It wasn't the blood that captured Sadie's attention, but the geometry of the angles and shapes JJ made up. With his ankles tied together and legs flat on the ground and his upper body tied to the shelves he mirrored the angles of the fallen shelves. His arms were tied away from his sides as if in crucifixion or a cruel imitation of the Y from the YMCA song and dance. But most captivating to Sadie was the soft triangle of dark hair on his naked chest. Or was it the shape of a heart Sadie wondered to herself.

"Help me with his legs, lift them as high as you can," Olive said.

Still wondering about shapes Sadie helped Olive and together the struggled to lift JJ's legs. After a few moments, Sadie's arms and shoulders reminded her that she had never practiced the squat or shoulder press in the gym, and they began shaking under the strain. JJ groaned and Olive said she could drop the legs saving her from explaining she couldn't hold them any longer. None too gently she dropped JJ's legs as Olive also let go.

The rough treatment caused JJ to groan again, and his eye's flickered but didn't open and his head lolled to the side again. Abruptly Olive stepped forward and smacked JJ hard across the face. The crack of the slap felt personal despite the violence of earlier and moved Sadie to reprimand Olive.

"Olive, how could you?" Sadie heard herself say in a scolding tone alien even to herself.

"Needs must, my dear, needs must," Olive muttered still focused on JJ.

JJ appeared to resuscitate under the administration of the slap. Blearily blinking he took in his surroundings and his own position. Then he began shouting spittle flying from his face.

"What the fuck did you do to me? Did you cut up my t-shirt? You stupid bitch. I'll kill you for that. I'll make you pay once I get out of here."

Sadie shrank back under the tirade, but Olive stood calmly, ignoring the abuse. Olive then pulled out the switch blade from her bag that she still had hooked in one arm.

"You won't be getting out of here any time soon," Olive said as she casually flicked the knife open.

Fear momentarily appeared on JJ's face as the knife reflected the light, but then bravado stamped it out.

"You wouldn't dare," he said puffing out his chest.

"Tell me what is going on here," Olive said, ignoring his statement, "What are you doing where? Why the library? What do you hope to achieve?"

"I'm not telling you shit."

"We don't have time for your attitude, I need results," Olive said in a manner of fact voice and stepped forward. With one hand she drove the blade all the way to the hilt into the meat of JJ's leg while with the other she muffled JJ's scream.

The sight of this wanton violence from someone she thought was a gentle old woman was too much for Sadie. She felt the blood rush from her head and the floor reach up to grab her as darkness crept into her vision. Before she blacked out completely Sadie heard Olive's voice one more time.

"For fuck's sake."

A giggle sprouted in Sadie's belly to hear Olive curse, but it was swallowed quickly in the darkness.

Chapter 51

There wasn't a dish out of place in the kitchen when Miriam arrived home mid-afternoon. A note on the kitchen table told her the kids would be back at six o'clock in plenty of time before the party and that the catering company confirmed they would deliver at seven thirty.

Miriam sighed with pleasure as she relished the silence of the house before the evening kicked off. She wandered into the spacious dining room nodding in approval at the extra table ready for the food. Nothing was left to chance, she noted, as little jugs of colourful flowers were dotted around the room. The kids had ordered a selection of hot food, Bain maries already set up on one table, and salads and various breads and rolls on the other. Nothing too fancy, just good, tasty food.

She kicked off her shoes and ambled out to the patio, keen to get the full effect for the party. The bar that Pete had been working on for days looked fantastic. It was painted jet black with ropes of lights curled around the edges and draped across the top bar. A bowl of lemons and a sharp knife lay on the left-hand side alongside an ice bucket ready for service. Wine glasses hung from the overhead top rung.

So clever, she thought. Ciaran will be impressed. He had been disappointed when Pete showed no interest in joining the Guards or going to university when he finished secondary school. He was never an enthusiastic student but had achieved a pretty good Leaving Cert and he knew he wanted to work with his hands and his brain. His two sisters went to college and loved it. Pete had always been the creative one and chose a carpentry apprenticeship.

"If that's what you want then go for it," his dad told him. "Sure, wasn't my own father a carpenter so it must be in the blood. And a good one he was too but, in those days, you just learned on the job." Miriam expected he would get a lot of orders from friends tonight when they saw the fabulous bar.

She reached up and took a wine glass from the rack and padded back into the kitchen to get a bottle of Sauvignon Blanc from the fridge. Back in the garden she unscrewed the top, poured herself a generous measure and sat back in the evening sun. Lights drooped from tree to tree and among the shrubs. She couldn't wait to see the full effect when the light started to fade later. The little red shiny hearts scattered on every table glistened in the sun. As she sipped, she reflected that things just couldn't be better. Today seemed to be a day for reflection. She wondered if Ciaran was feeling the same. She looked at her watch and realised it was almost time for him to be home. No point in phoning. He'd be on his way now.

An hour later and no word from Ciaran. Where the hell was he? She tried his mobile phone. It was turned off. This was not like Ciaran. He'd always text or phone if he was going to be late. She had always tried to minimise the risks involved in police work, but it could be dangerous, particularly in the city. Thank God Newbridge is a quiet enough town, but you never know, she thought. She tried Ciaran's phone again. Nothing.

Miriam wasn't a fusser, generally speaking. She was a practical woman who believed that there was no point in worrying needlessly. It was a waste of time and energy. 'Take your own advice for once. He'll be home soon', she reprimanded herself.

As time marched on, her phone staying stubbornly silent, her mind went into overdrive. The prevalence of drugs and violence and gangland murders were part of everyday life now. Was it last week that a small town in the midland had two murders in the one household? And she knew from Ciaran that gangland feuds have spiralled and spilled out into the suburbs. Wasn't Newbridge like a suburb of Dublin now? Like a slow tide rushing along the pebbles of a beach, anxiety turned to fear as she felt in her gut something was wrong.

Hands trembling, she tried phoning Newbridge Garda station. It was engaged. Calm down, she told herself. He'll be home any minute now. She'd have her shower while she waited. It would calm her. She was letting her imagination run riot. She threw her mobile on the bed, stripped off and wrapped a large towel around her.

She flicked on the TV news and was about to step into the en suite when swirling blue lights flashing on the TV screen caught her eye. RTE's crime reporter was standing in front of the camera with a microphone clutched in his hand. Behind him were Garda cars and vans, ambulances and a mass of Gardai surrounding a building. She turned the sound up as the reporter dramatically reported an armed hold up in Newbridge where hostages had been taken. She flopped down on the bed, her eyes scanning the screen for Ciaran.

The drama of the scene was reflected in the urgency of the reporter's tone of voice.

"It's a tense situation here in Newbridge. We understand that a shot was heard from inside the library about 45 minutes ago where a group of at least six people are being held hostage. It is understood that one of the hostages has been injured and Gardai are negotiating on the phone with one of the armed hostage takers. An ambulance and medics are on alert.

The background to the hostage taking would appear to be that two raiders held up a bookies shop in Newbridge town and were foiled in their attempt to escape. It is thought they entered the library to gain cover and discovered a writing group were meeting in the building. This is Derby Day, the highlight of the Curragh's racing calendar in Kildare. Roads in and out of Newbridge have been blocked and traffic is being diverted. The names of the hostages have not yet been released."

The piercing tone of Miriam's phone ringing startled her. 'Thank God,' she whispered as she grabbed it off the bed almost toppling in the process. "Have you heard from dad, mom?" shouted Pete, clearly phoning from his car. "Is he home yet?"

She slumped forward hardly able to reply with disappointment that it wasn't Ciaran. "I thought it was dad phoning me, Pete. Oh, dear God, I'm watching the news, and it doesn't look good. He should have been home ages ago and I haven't heard from him. I can't get through to his phone or the station. I don't know what to do, what to think." The tremor in her voice, normally so calm and reassuring, was alarming.

"Look mom. I'll head over to Newbridge and try and find out what's happening. Maybe I'll get to speak to someone who knows if dad is OK."

"I don't think you'll get very far Pete. It says on the news that all roads into and out of Newbridge are blocked. Can you think of anyone else in the station that we could phone?"

"I can't think offhand mom. I'll come over straight away and I'll phone the girls. We'll all be there shortly. Try to keep calm." Miriam knew Pete meant well and was as worried as she was. The only thing that would calm her was to see Ciaran walk through the hall door. She put her head in her hands and sobbed.

Chapter 52

DCI Barry, DCI Darcy, Sergeant Moore and Sergeant Daly all came to the same conclusion. It was time to put an end to the hostage situation.

"We're ready to go in now," Sergeant Daly confirmed.

"Hang on," Sergeant Moore argued, "just a bit longer."

"We've waited long enough."

DCI Darcy looked up, surprised at the sharp tone of the usually quiet-spoken, endlessly patient, Bill Daly.

"Don't look at me like that, Ciaran," Bill shook his head. "This has gone on long enough. It's time to put an end to it."

The ragtime ring tone of DCI Barry's phone caught them all off guard and set them all laughing.

"A sure tension breaker," DCI Barry smiled as he walked away, his mobile to his ear.

"Why wait, Tom?" Ciaran asked his second in command.

"He gave us two hours, remember. We can ask for another hour at least. Tell them the traffic from the Derby is mayhem. Traffic jams all the way to Dublin. That would give us extra time to figure out another way in there."

"We know there's only one way in," Bill Daly said, "we've been over this a hundred times."

"I'd lay odds there's at least one tunnel under that building. We need to talk to Mario Corrigan or James Durney."

DCI Ciaran Darcy nodded. As usual Tom had come up with a good suggestion. It sounded like a workable alternative, and one that might save lives if the hostage takers got trigger happy. He looked over at DCI Barry whose phone call had ended but obviously had given him something to think about.

"Anything we should know?" he said.

"Definitely," DCI Barry tapped the phone off his hand as he walked back to the waiting, curious group.

"We've found our mole," DCI Barry put his phone back in his breast pocket.

DCI Ciaran Darcy felt his heart miss a beat. Up until that moment he was convinced that the mole was just a figment of the super's imagination. Ever since it had first been suggested to him that there was a leak, he went through every single interaction he had with those around him. He had known Bill Daly for years. They had first worked together on hostage situation down in Kilkenny years ago and their paths had crossed several times since. Bill knew no other way of life. His father was a Garda. Bill went straight into Templemore from school. He met his wife there. Darcy was sure the mole couldn't be Bill Daly.

As for Tom Moore, DCI Darcy had come to rely on Tom over the past ten years. He was quiet, reserved yet extremely observant. Tom knew everything about everybody yet gave very little away about his life outside the station. The source of Tom's obvious wealth did cross his mind years earlier when he was first stationed in Newbridge, but he was reliably informed that the money came from Tom's wife. A socialite, daughter of one of the most successful and wealthiest solicitors in the entire country. There could be no reason for Tom Moore to turn rogue.

"Your badge, Tom." DCI Barry held out his hand.

Shock froze DCI Darcy and he audibly gasped.

"I don't fucking believe it," Bill Daly turned pointedly and stared at Tom Moore, the surprise evident in his tone. "You're the mole!"

Tom Moore's face and neck turned beetroot and he blustered.

"Don't be ridiculous. You can't make an allegation like that. I'll have you know, I'm very well respected in this district. A mole, that's ludicrous," Tom guffawed.

"How many hostages are injured Tom," DCI Barry's tone brokered no argument.

"What? What are you talking about?"

"How many hostages are injured?"

"All of them, sure you told me that."

"Except I lied. I told Sergeant Daly a different number. Guess which number came back on the grapevine, Tom?"

"But...but...that's not proof, that's..."

"Don't even try to deny it," DCI Barry's clipped voice cut Tom Moore short, "it's all the proof I need for now, Tom. Your badge."

Tom Moore's eyes narrowed as he pulled himself up to his full height.

"I am not surrendering my badge. I've done nothing wrong."

"Where's your car, Moore,"

Moore's eyes widened, "My car, what do you want with my car?"

"I want to search it, Moore. I've reason to believe I may find the proceeds of a crime contained in it."

"Now you really are getting ridiculous. Ciaran, tell him. Tell him I couldn't be a mole."

DCI Darcy stared at the man he had trusted completely until that moment. He knew instinctively that DCI Barry was right. Moore was their mole.

A quick search of Tom Moore's car unearthed the evidence they needed. Ten thousand euros in fifty-euro notes hidden in the cars tool compartment.

"That's my wife's money. She asked me to lodge it, but I didn't get a chance."

"And she will verify that will she?" DCI Darcy took out his phone as he spoke, "hi, Stephanie, Ciaran Darcy here…Yes, all good, looking forward to the party. Listen, I hate to disturb you, but Tom's been called away so didn't get to the bank. I'm putting the cash in the hold here in the station for safekeeping, but I need to log it. How much is in it?"

"I see."

"Ahh, maybe I picked him up wrong. That's grand, Stephanie. Don't worry about it. Talk to you later."

DCI Darcy hung up and stared at his Sergeant.

"Funny that. Stephanie doesn't know anything about it."

The colour leaked from Tom Moore's face. His usual ruddy complexion turning grey starting from his forehead down. He hung his head.

"Murry, Thomson," DCI Barry called two uniformed Garda, "please escort Mr Tom Moore to the station. Lock him in the cells until I can get there."

Chapter 53

The clock mounted on the wall of the delivery suite told Marie she'd been in the hospital almost two hours, though it felt like much longer. The time between her contractions was dropping slowly but surely and while the baby wasn't ready to come just yet, she was sure it wouldn't be too much longer.

She winced as yet another wave of pain flooded through her body, and she grabbed a nearby plastic device, sucking in a mouthful of gas and air. Ten seconds passed, then fifteen, and the pain began to subside.

Marie lay back in the bed and checked her phone, her heart dropping when she saw no new messages or missed calls. She'd phoned Larry so many times in the last few hours that her call log was just a long list of his name, repeated over and over. She wondered where the hell he was. What on earth was he doing that was so important he couldn't be here at the hospital with her? She needed him now more than ever.

Marie didn't think she could get through this on her own. Larry was all she had. Her parents had died years ago, when she was still in school, and as an only child she'd been left on her own to make her way through the world. Two years later, Larry came along, and he'd been by her side ever since. Until now.

Marie blinked back tears and forced a smile on her face as the midwife strode into the room, enquired as to how she was feeling, used a small handheld device to examine the baby's heart rate, then checked to see how dilated Marie was. The woman was in her mid-forties, with a friendly but no-nonsense manner about her.

"Just over four centimetres," the midwife said as she straightened up. "Not quite there just yet. We'll have another look in an hour."

Marie flashed her a watery smiled and turned her head to look out the window. From where she was lying all she could see was an endless expanse of blue sky, the city of Kilkenny hidden from view.

Her phone began to buzz, and she almost dropped it on the floor. Larry's name was flashing across the screen, and she quickly swiped to answer him.

"Where the hell are you?" was the first thing she said. "You know I'm down in the hospital, right? This baby's on the way and you're nowhere to be seen. What're you doing? Why haven't you been answering your calls or texts?"

There was a pause on the other end of the line. "I'm really sorry, Marie, I never meant for any of this. I'm – it's... I can't exactly explain what's going on, but I'm going to do my very best to get down to you as soon as I can, okay?"

Marie shook her head. "I knew it. It's something to do with your brother, am I right? What's he got you involved in now? What are you doing for him?"

There was another pause. She could hear him swallowing.

"I'm... caught up in something here," he conceded. "It's a bit hairy, I won't lie. But I'm going to get out of it. I've thought of a way. How're you doing? Is everything okay?"

"Just get down here," Marie snapped, her tone harsher than she meant. "Look, I'm okay, everything's okay with the baby so far, but it's coming, d'you understand? I need you here with me. I can't do this on my own."

There was a shout in the background, a man's voice, then the sound of a woman swearing.

"I'm sorry," Larry said quickly. "I've got to go. I love you."

And he hung up.

Chapter 54

'Kids today have no backbone,' Olive thought to herself and continued her exploration of the basement leaving Sadie and JJ behind. "They're so fragile, a bit of light torture and JJ broke easily, and poor Sadie had no stomach to even watch.'

At least she had gotten what she wanted quickly from JJ, and it didn't need to get messy. It was obvious that he was hired muscle and didn't know much. What he did know was that it was more than a theft gone wrong. The Carpenter was involved somehow, Olive was no expert on him, but organised crime involvement was never good. She needed to call DCI Ciaran Darcy and fill him in on the bit she knew.

There was no phone coverage down in the basement though, so she needed to either find an exit out of the basement or risk going back up into the library. To make matter worse her phone just buzzed to let her know that she only had 20% battery left. Olive set it to power saver and continued her search through the maze of shelves. The growing layers of dust on everything Olive disturbed in her passing told her that no one had ventured this far into the back of the basement in a long time. She felt she would soon either find an exit or an end to the basement. She hoped that her gut feeling was right that a basement this large had to have more than a single entrance and exit, but then again it was built before health and safety became what it is today.

There was a subtle change to the next row of shelves Olive came face to face with. It took a few strides of walking beside them before she could put her finger on what it was. The depth was wrong, there was a solid wall behind shelves, the shadows made them seem shallower. She had found the end of the basement. She just needed to find a corner and then retrace her steps back the other direction and she would know for sure if there was a door here or not.

Olive's searching was quickly rewarded, but it wasn't a door as she expected but a sturdy looking metal gate with an oversize padlock. Behind the gate she could see a hallway leading to what looked like stairs. The light from her phone wasn't enough to illuminate everything at the end of the hall, but Olive was satisfied she had found an exit. More than that potentially an exit unknown to those upstairs and the Garda. This unnecessarily secure gate was the only hurdle stopping her from confirming and getting the precious phone cover she needed. Sometimes function and the desire to use up public budget at the end of a year resulted in some interesting purchase, Olive thought, otherwise this basement housed something more important than dust. But now wasn't the time for that particular mystery as Olive dug out some hair pins from her bag. After straightening them out and pulling the rubber end of the metal with her teeth, Olive inserted one into the lock firmly while she gently searched for the pins in the lock with the other. Ten frustration minutes later Olive was still twisting and turning the hair pins having made no progress.

Olive still had no phone coverage, and the battery was now down to 18%. It was time for a decision, keep trying the door and potentially run out of battery before making it out or risk going back up into the library. Going back into the library felt the better decision, if she couldn't call, at least she could hide and send off some text messages, down here she was achieving nothing more. Ciaran Darcy could probably find this entrance and make short work on the gate with the right tools. Decision made Olive tried to trace her way back to Sadie, JJ and the trapdoor to the library. It was easy going following her footsteps which stood out like beacons in the disturbed dust.

Chapter 55

Sadie tasted bile in her mouth as she lay on the cold floor breathing heavily through her mouth. She wasn't so naive as to think this was all a horrible nightmare that she will wake up from, but she really wished she was. She had woken up today looking forward to writing group, she had a new piece they were going to critique, and she was excited to hear the feedback. It's not easy exposing yourself and putting your words forward for others to review but the buzz afterwards always pushed her on. Afterwards she had planned to reward herself with a relaxing coffee in Whitewater with a bit of people watching and then plan the rest of her day. Instead, she was in the musty basement with a childhood crush turned violent criminal in some mad hostage situation.

Sitting up gingerly Sadie ran her finger through her hair, doing her best not to breathe through her nose. The mix of smells didn't bare thinking about if she was going to pull herself together.

The light from the mobile phone on the ground allowed her to take in her surroundings. JJ was still tied up and seeing the knife sticking from his leg Sadie remembered the scene of Olive stabbing him with a jolt. Sadie screwed her eyes shut as she relived the scene, the awful soft thump at the knife sank to the hilt in JJ's flesh. Should it not have been a wet sound with all the blood, Sadie though. With a shudder Sadie opened her eyes, she needed to distract herself from this thinking.

"Where's Olive?" she asked JJ.

"That crazy bitch, she has gone further into the back. Who is she?"

Some of the bravado was back in JJ's voice but Sadie could still hear the echo of the pain and fear from when Olive had stabbed him.

Who was Olive was a good question, Sadie thought. Olive had been one of the lovely ladies in her writing group that wrote fantastic action scenes with bad ass heroines. It was as if Olive had morphed into one of the characters from her stories except no one had told her that she is in her sixties and there are no heroes in real life. There are no hero's or villains in real life, nothing is that black and white, everything is a mix of depressing grey. A moan of pain broke through the wall of JJ's bravado interrupting Sadie's thoughts. Like a damn bursting JJ started shivering and muttering to himself. Listening closely without moving Sadie could just make out what he was muttering over and over to himself.

"She stabbed me, she stabbed me. How could she? She really stabbed me."

He's in shock with the pain, Sadie thought, hell, I am in shock myself. Maybe I should help him? The poor guy is in a lot of pain. What? Are you fucking crazy, this is the guy that took you hostage. Yes, but he was a good kid when you knew him, didn't you just say that everything is a grey? We should at least help him with the pain.

Fuck him, fuck grey and fuck the pain, this is the guy that punched lovable old Maxwell, he desires the pain.

No one desires pain! Maybe he is just misunderstood, don't add yourself to, what is probably a long list of people to misunderstand him. Give him a second chance!

Fuck that, he can have his second chance after we get out of here and he does his prison time.

Who are you to deny someone a second chance, where would you be without your second chance? Beside maybe he can get you out of here, you had a lot of influence over him as a kid, maybe you can use some of that influence now, convince him to free everyone.

Sadie felt very strange as she watched herself argue with herself, almost as if she had split herself into three, and hovered above herself as she watched the images of herself argue back and forth. She noticed with a shadow of smile that part of her had a foul mouth.

With an effort of imagination Sadie pulled herself together and got to her feet.

"Let me take out the knife, it might help with the pain."

"NO." JJ yelled scaring Sadie back a step.

"If you take it out, I could bleed to death. At least that's what the crazy bitch said," JJ said terror piecing every note. Looking again, Sadie could see a cloth tourniquet around his left leg and the handle of the knife but very little blood. "I don't want to die, please help me."

"Why should I, you took me and my friend's hostage?"

"I was forced to, this wasn't my plan, this was all Larry's fault. He got me caught up in this mess. It was meant to be an easy inside job where I pick up some cash from the bookies. Then the shit goes sideways, and we end up in this fucked up library. The really fucked up part that Larry was hiding from me is that The Carpenter is involved. That means we ARE all fucked. Me most of all, and on top of that I have this bitch craving me up in the basement."

"Who is The Carpenter?"

"You don't know who The Carpenter is? He is the dude you don't want to fuck with. You cross him and you will quickly find yourself in a coffin. A closed coffin cause he will fuck you up real bad first. That's why they call him The Carpenter. You've got to help me."

"What will you do if I help you?"

"Get the fuck out of here!" Sadie could hear the genuine panic in voice. "And bring you with me of course," JJ added as an afterthought.

The idea of escape and getting out of here was so sweet that Sadie found herself reaching for the knots at his wrists before she could stop herself.

"Quickly, I think I hear her coming back," JJ whispered spurring Sadie on.

Chapter 56

Olive felt her pace quickening as she followed her footsteps in the dust back to Sadie. She had to force herself to slow down, she needed to remain cautious, particularly now that she could see an end to this mess. Her adrenaline was up but she needed to remain composed and not make any mistakes. She just needed to get back to the trapdoor and the library above, she could then contact Ciaran and tell them about the entrance. A quick look at council records for the building and they would find the entrance, then it was just a matter of storming in and taking the last criminal by surprise. Olive felt a little bubble of satisfaction in her chest, she had taken out one of the criminals by herself. She couldn't wait to see Ciaran's face, he will splutter and spit about the danger, her age and that she shouldn't be taking those risks, but she knew he would be secretly impressed that she still had it.

Olive just needed a bit of luck and for her phone battery to last, even just enough to send of a text message. A quick glance at her phone showed Olive that she was down to 15%, that should be enough, but then again sometimes her battery just decided that enough was enough and died despite having a percentage left. Once that battery colour went yellow, it was her signal that the phone could die at any minute.

Olive rounded the latest corner around the shelves and was taken by surprise to have arrived back with Sadie and JJ. She berated herself silently for having gotten lost in her own thoughts. The one consolation was that Sadie and JJ seemed to be equally surprised at her arrival back. Sadie had been bending over JJ and jumped back in surprise, her face flushing red as she continued to shuffle backwards.

That girl is too gentle, Olive thought and not for the first time, life is going to eat Sadie without salt if she doesn't harden up a little. Sadie must have been over trying to comfort JJ. That girl would take in a rabid dog after it bite her rather than putting it down.

Sadie was clearly embarrassed about her behaviour, so rather than quizzing her on what she was doing Olive moved on to more important matters.

"I have found a way-out Sadie. I can't unlock it, but if I can get back upstairs where I have phone coverage, I can contact the Guard's and they can put a quick end to all this."

Surprisingly, Sadie appeared more panicked than comforted at Olive's words.

"Chin up girl, I won't get caught going upstairs, just sit tight and this will all be over soon. I'll just check the knots on this guy first and then I will be as quick as I can," Olive said as she moved to check JJ's bonds.

"Wait." Sadie squealed, the force behind that single word caused Olive to turn her head to Sadie.

Olive felt a whoosh of air on her ear, followed by an explosion of pain across her temple, then nothing.

***

"Jesus." Sadie murmured in shock as she watched Olive crumple to the floor.

"What have you done?" she said, her voice growing in power. "What the actual fuck have you done?"

"Shut up and use your pretty little head for a minute," JJ snapped, "What do you think this bitch would have done to you when she found you have untied me? You loosen the knot enough that I could get my hand out and I took the swing before she could."

Sadie deflated like a punctured tires under this logic.

"Now come over here and untie me the rest of the way. I am going to need your help to walk and get back upstairs. Then Larry will be able to get us out of here."

Numbly Sadie did as she was told, making sure not to look at where Olive lay still on the ground.

As she got JJ on his feet, and they started hobbling back to the stairs she could help but think what she had done? Poor Olive. She was still alive right? She had to be. But she was old, old people can be frail. No, no, don't think like that, she is fine. I just need to get out of here, everything will be ok then, JJ will get me out of here and it will all be fine. This needs to end.

Chapter 57

Larry starred in disbelief at his phone. It's Ben, he thought, it can't be Ben. His hand shook as he answered the call.

"Hello?"

"Larry, it's me, Ben. Listen, Larry, I don't have much time. You have to go to the Gardai. Tell them The Carpenter is planning to kidnap John Magnier today, in the Curragh Racecourse. He's planning to escape by helicopter just after the last race. It's a Robinson R22."

"Ben, where are..."

"Later, Larry, I'll explain everything later. Just get to the Gardai, now, before it's too late."

Larry's mind raced. Ben didn't know that Larry was holed up in the library holding hostages. Who could have foreseen that? He clapped a hand to his forehead. Or is that what this was all about? Is that why the Gardai arrived so quickly trapping them in here. Did The Carpenter tip them off about a robbery on the Main Street? A diversion. This was his chance to redeem himself. He lifted the phone.

"Hello."

DCI Darcy's voice held a note of surprise, "Hello."

"I have information for you, but you need to act on it quickly. The Carpenter is planning to kidnap John Magnier in the Curragh

Racecourse today. His helicopter is waiting to lift him out of there shortly. It's a Robinson R22. You need to intercept him before it's too late."

"How do you know...."

"I'll explain later. Stop him first," Larry hung up. His mind raced. Where the hell is Ben. If they caught The Carpenter, what did that mean for him. Could he possibly get out of this mess?

"What's going on?" Betty asked.

"They don't have my brother anymore. He's free."

"Who doesn't have your brother?"

"The Carpenter."

"Who?"

Larry clapped his hands together and beamed at his hostages.

"I think we can help each other."

"You're sadly mistaken if you think we're going to help you in any way," Siobhan said, two pink spots high on her cheekbones.

"I don't blame you, but please, hear me out."

Larry pulled a chair over to the table beside them.

"What has your brother got to do with it?" Betty asked. Larry looked at Betty's face and saw his own mirrored there. He sighed, trying to figure out how to explain how this group of people ended up as hostages in the library of all places.

"My brother Ben...well he got into trouble. He's not a bad lad, just got in with the wrong crowd, he owed money to a gang run by a guy called The Carpenter. Dangerous fella. Anyway, when Ben told me I didn't know what to do."

Larry hesitated unsure how much he should say.

Betty encouraged him, "Go on, what did you do?"

"Ben is adopted. We both are," he glanced at Betty. "It was Ben's birth mother that got him into drugs in the first place. Money was no object with her. She spent her weekends snorting cocaine, drinking Bollinger and generally living the high life on her husband's money."

"So… you sent Ben to her?" Siobhan asked.

"Yes, big mistake," Larry shook his head. "She handed him over to her dealer who handed him to The Carpenter. Along with the information that I manage the bookies across the road."

"You manage a betting shop?" Siobhan sounded incredulous.

"Yep, believe it or not. I manage a betting shop. I'm married with a baby on the way, any day now. My wife has been ringing me all day and I can't answer her because I don't know what to do. I don't know how to get out of this." A note of panic sounded in Larry's voice. "I didn't want to get involved. They gave me no choice."

"Why don't you tell us what happened, Larry," Betty said.

Grateful for the sympathetic tone, Larry did as Betty instructed. Composing himself, he took a deep breath and started again.

"You see, I got a call... from The Carpenter. He said they had Ben, and they would kill him if I didn't do what he said."

"What did he want you to do?" Betty asked.

"He said that I was to let his guy rob the betting shop on Derby Saturday. Fill his rucksack and let him out without raising the alarm." The words spilled out of Larry's mouth, "But... you see, Charlie, my boss, he trusts me. This job has changed my life. We're saving for a mortgage, and we've a baby on the way. I couldn't let my boss down, but I couldn't let them kill Ben. My parents would never forgive me. They think little enough of me as it is."

"So... what are you saying?" Maxwell interrupted, "You decided to rob the betting shop yourself?"

"No... no of course not. But when JJ came into the betting shop, well let's face it, he's not the brightest. So, I had this brainwave. I thought that if I took the rucksack, pretended to him that I was part of the robbery, then maybe I could save Ben and keep Charlie's money, that if I didn't let the money out of my sight and managed to return it then Charlie would never know."

"Not very joined up thinking," Siobhan said, looking at Larry from under her glasses like a schoolteacher talking to an errant pupil.

"No, I realise that. Honestly, I don't know what I was thinking," Larry said. "The minute we got outside it went pear shaped. I presumed JJ had a getaway car outside. I mean these are supposed to be a professional gang. But no, JJ was on foot. Next thing I know somebody's shouting stop thief and there's a uniformed Gardai chasing us. JJ ran and I followed him. This was the first open door we came to."

"So, you didn't intend to take hostages," Maxwell said.

"No, of course not. This has been a bloody disaster. What the hell were you doing here on a Saturday afternoon anyway."

"We're a writer's group, Larry. We meet here on Saturday afternoons once a month."

Larry gestured to his back pocket. "I'm going to take the knife out of my pocket and cut you all loose. Okay?"

A unison of okays followed. Betty put her hand on Larry's arm. "You should ring your wife."

"And tell her what?"

"Tell her you love her."

Larry smiled, "she knows that." But he did what Betty advised.

"Marie?"

"Larry, where the hell are you?"

Larry cringed at the anger in her voice.

"You need to get to the hospital. Now."

Larry stared at the phone in his hand, his mouth open, his heart racing into his throat.

"My wife is about to give birth. I have to get out...."

"Look who I found," JJ's singsong tone silenced Larry.

"What the...?"

Sadie held up a bedraggled JJ, a bloodied knife visibly sticking out of his upper left leg. Pushing Sadie to one side he limped over to Larry.

"We're getting out of here. Now," JJ said, "Where's the backpack?"

"Hold up, JJ. We're surrounded. There's no way out."

"Look what she did to me. That bloody lunatic, she thought she could truss me up like a bloody chicken but lookie here, I'm still standing. Where's the bitch now?"

The hairs stood up on Larry's head at the implication of JJ's words.

"Who, JJ. Who did that to you?"

"That ole wan. I shut her up."

"What did you do, JJ?"

Larry's rush of hope got punched full force. He felt it drain out of him, flushed away by JJ's slack mouthed grin.

"I'm getting out of here. You can come with or stay. I don't care either way, but I'm taking the money. Now give it to me."

Larry reached behind the desk for the backpack and fired it at JJ. It landed two feet in front of him. JJ's manic laughter sounded surreal in the normally sedate library. Larry shuddered. This day was getting worse by the second. JJ laughing his head off like some cheap evil villain in a 50s thriller, their hostages sitting around the table like they were at a school meeting. Maxwell with his eyes closed. Siobhan cowering as if in anticipation of a hard punch, Betty, open mouthed yet glued to his every facial expression. Daniel was clutching the arms of his chair so tightly his knuckles had turned white.

"If you want to walk out that door, it's fine by me," Larry said.

"I never mentioned walking out the door. I'm not a total gobshite. There's a bloody tunnel. In the basement."

Larry registered the look on Betty's face. She knew about it. Maybe he did have a chance of getting to Marie. If he ran now. Problem was he didn't want to associate himself with JJ, any further than he already was. A few minutes ago, he had the semblance of an escape plan. Now his escape plan mean following JJ and he wasn't sure that was a good idea.

Daniel stood, still gripping the chair and propelled himself backwards, knocking an unstable JJ to the floor, screaming in pain.

Sadie screamed, "Stop it, stop, can't you see he's injured."

"What's the matter with you. He's a lunatic." Siobhan shook Sadie by the shoulders as Maxwell and Daniel wrestled with JJ. Daniel tied his wrists behind his back, ignoring his screams. "Call the Garda, Betty," Siobhan said.

"Are we all agreed that Larry here needs to get out of here before that happens?" Betty looked at each one of them eye to eye.

Siobhan shook her head, "No, woah, right there." She pointed an accusatory finger at Larry. "He held us captive. He threatened us. Do you honestly believe he should walk away free?"

"But Siobhan, in fairness, Larry told us what happened," Maxwell said, "I don't think he's bad, he was put in an impossible situation. None of us know how we would react if we were in his shoes."

"If it makes you feel any better, Siobhan, our plan is to get Larry to see his baby being born. He can suffer the consequences of his actions afterwards," Betty clarified.

"It's not up for discussion," Siobhan practically stamped her feet, "There's no excuse. He could have gone to the Gardai about his brother. He could have spoken to his boss. But he didn't. How do you know he's telling you the truth about his brother? He could be spinning you all the biggest yarn and you fell for it?"

Daniel stood up beside Siobhan. "Siobhan's right. We don't know this guy from Adam. He told us he was only supposed to allow the robbery to go ahead without calling the Gardai. What did he do? He stole that money himself. I smell a rat?"

Betty moved quickly. She lifted a small white cloth bag from the side of the counter, grabbed Larry by the arm and pushed him out of the main library and towards the corridor.

"Quick, follow me."

Shocked into action, Larry blindly followed her as she fumbled in the bag, pulled out an ancient looking key and raced towards the trapdoor. Larry followed, rendered speechless by this turn of events. He followed Betty blindly down the steps into the basement. She flicked on a switch and a dull light flickered overhead.

"It's a labyrinth down here. It hasn't been used in years. I just hope I can remember the way."

"Wait," Larry did his best to hide the entrance, pulling the carpet back down over it before closing and bolting the trapdoor. "It might give us a few extra minutes."

They hurried along until they met a junction. Two identical corridors, both in darkness.

"I don't know," Betty's voice jittered, "I can't remember."

Larry flicked on the torch on his phone.

"No need to, look," Larry pointed at the dusty footprints emerging from the right corridor, "That has to be the way."

"I'm nearly sure this tunnel comes out at the river, at the Athgarvan side of the Liffey Linear Park."

"You knew this tunnel was here the whole time?"

"They were built during the Civil war, escape routes for anti-treaty fighters held captive in Newbridge barracks. They were maintained for a while but then budget restraints put a stop to that. I'd forgotten about them to be honest. And then when I did remember, I was afraid this one would be such a state of disrepair it would have collapsed."

Betty looked doubtfully at the tunnel entrance.

"How do you know it hasn't?"

Betty shook her head, "Immaterial. The point is: Larry, this is your chance to escape. If it doesn't work out, you can turn back. Let's go."

They hadn't gone very far when they heard a low moaning.

"Listen, it must be Olive. That eejit JJ hurt her."

Larry hurried his steps with Betty following closely. They found her propped up against the wall, holding her head in her hands and moaning softly like an injured cat. Betty touched Larry's arm and put her forefinger to her lips to silence him.

"Go, quickly. I'll see to her. You need to get out of here."

Larry hesitated but Betty pushed him. "Go, don't miss the birth of your son."

Chapter 58

The Carpenter pushed his way through the crowd, eyes cast down as he made for the nearest exit. The Curragh Racecourse was thronged with people strutting around in their Sunday best, blissfully unaware of the drama unfolding underneath their noses. The Carpenter sidestepped a swaying, suited teenager, praying he hadn't been spotted.

How quickly events had spiralled out of control. In one moment, he was invincible, his plan being executed to perfection, his Caribbean Island closer than it had ever been. The next – disaster. Someone must have talked, he realised, there was no other explanation. Someone had betrayed him. He cursed them as he walked, cursed whoever had turned on him, but cursed himself too. He should never have come here in the first place. He'd only survived this long in this line of work by staying away from the frontline, conducting his twisted orchestra from a distance. It had been his golden rule, the only rule to remain unbroken, the only line to remain uncrossed. A sudden shiver ran down his spine at the thought of making it so close to the end only to fail at the final hurdle.

With an effort, The Carpenter forced himself to focus on the here and now. There would be time for reflection and bone breaking later. Right this moment, he needed to get as far away from the racecourse as possible.

He risked a glance over his shoulder. The plainclothes detectives weren't far behind but hadn't seen him yet. Steel-eyed with close-cropped hair, they wore earpieces and scanned the crowds. He looked over to the stands where a line of uniformed gardaí had appeared just minutes earlier. Joseph, his second in command, had disappeared after shouting a warning, presumably hauled off for percussive questioning out of sight. The Carpenter could only assume the rest of his men had been caught too. He would have to rely on his own wits to get out of this one.

He stayed moving forward, forcing himself to walk slowly and keep his expression neutral. He knew nothing would capture the gardaí's eye more than someone hurrying through the crowds. The nearest exit was barely 20 metres away now. Close by in the car park was his Range Rover. He wouldn't be able to go back to his house, not now, but he could lie low at the safehouse in Swords for a few days, longer if necessary. A trip, under cover of darkness, over the border into Northern Ireland would follow when the heat had died down a little. Then a private boat from the seaside town of Ballycastle across to Scotland and a five-hour journey to a small airfield near Inverness where a private plane was waiting to whisk him away to another life.

Just as a little pep returned to The Carpenter's step, several more figures in uniform appeared, blocking his path to the Range Rover, and his heart sank. He looked back again for the men in plainclothes and froze as one of them caught his eye. Time seemed to stand still as they stared at one another, then a look of recognition flitted across the man's face and his eyes widened.

The Carpenter reacted first. He sprinted towards the racetrack, cries of surprise and anger ringing out as he shoved his way unceremoniously through the crowds. As he reached the white fence, he grunted as he was tackled from the side and hit the ground hard. He struggled, twisting and turning to break free, then cried out in pain as a knee drove into his spine and he was forced face first into the grass. His arms were wrenched backward, and his hands cuffed, then he was hauled to his knees.

"Bastards," he spat. Pain coursed through his nose; he knew it was broken. He could feel warm blood tricking down across his lips and a wave of fury and frustration washed over him. "You think you've got me? I'll get every one of you, believe me. We know where you live."

"And I know where you'll be living for the next twenty years," a voice called out from nearby.

"O'Shea," The Carpenter said, injecting as much venom as he could into every syllable. "Is that you?" A middle-aged man with a receding hairline and a broad grin stepped into his eyeline. The epaulettes on his shoulders marked him as a superintendent.

The Carpenter spat; a globule of blood-streaked saliva landed near the man's polished black shoes. Superintendent O'Shea's right leg twitched, as though he wanted to repay the insult, but he just smiled at the man on the ground.

You'll not be able to wriggle your way out of this one," he said with relish, then glanced at the arresting garda. "Get him out of my sight."

Chapter 59

Larry turned to Betty, unsure how to express his feelings. Before today, he hadn't given a second thought to the woman who gave birth to him. Yet, here she was, looking at him with what could only be love in her eyes. She was helping him escape from a crazy situation without even querying why she should help someone who had held her hostage.

Some of the others certainly didn't want to help. Betty initially looked for their agreement that they help him get out to get to the hospital in time for the birth, but it wasn't forthcoming. Betty, in her wisdom, didn't argue with them after that. But when the opportunity arose, she grabbed it with both hands.

"If ever I get out of this, I owe a huge debt to you," Larry said, taking Bettys hands, "Thank you, Betty."

Betty stroked his cheek with her right hand.

"I've always loved you; you know that don't you? You are always in my thoughts. Always have been and always will be."

"Betty, I...," the lump in Larry throat threatened to choke him. "Thank you...I don't know what else to say."

"Just go. We don't have time for sentimentality. You need to get out of here. Here, this is the key to the gate at the other end of the tunnel. There are my car keys. It's parked in The Gables car park. White polo. 151KE325.Go see that wife of yours. She needs you."

After a quick hug, Betty pushed Larry towards the tunnel and turned her attention to Olive who appeared to be coming around.

"I will be back. I have so many questions." Larry smiled before clambering into the tunnel. Within minutes he found himself in total black darkness. The surface beneath him felt like rotten undergrowth. The smell overpowered him at times. Fear kept him moving forward. If Olive went through this tunnel, so can I, he told himself. He reached the gate but managed to force it open with frantic kicks. He moved deeper into the darkness. Gradually the air around him felt fresher, the smell not so overpowering. Around him the blackness brightened to dusk. Ahead of him he could see light though a forest of greenery. His hand hit a wrought iron gate. The key was stiff in the lock, refusing to turn initially but he kept rattling it until he heard the click of the lock mechanism opening. The gate remained stubbornly closed.

"Christ," Larry exclaimed, "What the f..." He pushed hard. No give. If he could turn himself around, he could kick it out, but there wasn't enough room in the tunnel to turn his 6ft 2ins body. Summoning up every bit of strength he had left he pushed and kept pushing. The gate shifted slightly. He took a deep breath and pushed again. This time it burst out, getting tangled in the green froths in front of it.

A short drop brought him onto a bed of wild grasses. Larry took a minute to orientate himself. There were several families at various locations, sitting on benches, skimming stones in the river, kids riding bikes while parents walked with prams on the wide paths. He was struck by the normality of it all. A fine summer Saturday evening. He waited until the path nearest him cleared and made his way to path.

'Breathe Larry,' he told himself, 'Don't draw attention to yourself.'

He sauntered up the narrow path towards the carpark, making a concentrated effort to keep his pace slow and steady. The last thing he needed was to look like he was running away. The car was exactly where Betty said it would be. He nearly gave himself a hernia when he tried to get into the driver's seat and laughed out loud. Betty was a lot shorter than he was. The seat was pulled up as close to the windscreen as it would go. Larry could barely get the keys in the ignition his hands were shaking so much. After several deep breaths he managed it and the engine roared into life.

Larry turned left out the Athgarvan Road. To his right he could see the Gardai roadblock stopping every car that turned onto the road. He gave a silent prayer of thanks for Betty. When she told them that she parked in that car park and walked through the Liffey Linear Park to get to the library so she could avoid the traffic, Larry could have kissed her.

He looked at his watch. Forty minutes and he'd be in Portlaoise hospital with Marie. Please God, let me make it in time, he uttered a silent prayer as he put his foot on the accelerator.

Chapter 60

Daniel couldn't believe what he had just witnessed. Betty, the quiet unassuming librarian who had been so traumatised was helping one of their kidnappers get away.

"No Betty, get back here. You can't be serious."

"Go Larry, get out while you can," Maxwell said. Daniel looked at him in disbelief.

"Have you lost the plot?" Daniel said. Siobhan sided with Daniel.

Watching with increasing incredulity, JJ wriggled at the loose ties on his wrist. Larry had left the gun lying on the desk, unattended and unnoticed by the group. JJ pulled himself up and grabbed the gun.

"Shut up, the lot of ye." Pain shot through his leg as he struggled to stand upright. He gestured to Sadie who quickly stemmed the bleeding and put on a tourniquet. While Daniel admired her charitable spirit, he couldn't help feeling she could have done more to keep him immobilised rather than back in control with that gun in his hand.

"Get in front of that desk, now, all of you," JJ pushed Sadie back to the others.

Daniel watched with a growing unease as JJ paced back and forth across the library floor, gun in hand and clearly rattled. The young man was muttering to himself and was looking increasingly unhinged. Every few minutes, he made a burst for the main door or a nearby window, peeking around the coverings to see what the gardaí were up to.

Despite the medication he'd been given, a slight stab of pain suddenly coursed through Daniel's injured leg, and he winced in discomfort, shifting slightly where he sat to try and get more comfortable. His head was still sore too, and nausea swirled in his stomach, and he wondered if they were ever going to get out of this mess. If he made it out, he thought, he would ask the medics for the strongest painkillers they had then put him in a dark room where nobody could bother him.

JJ whirled at the slight noise of his movement and glared at Daniel.

"Don't move," he hissed at him, "None of you" – he brandished the gun in the direction of Maxwell and Siobhan too – "move an inch. If you do..." He trailed off, the weapon in his hand leaving none of them with any uncertainty as to their fate if they did so.

Maxwell waited until JJ had walked over to another window and tilted his head towards Daniel.

"I think we have to do something," he muttered, keeping one eye on JJ who was peering through the blinds. "This guy looks like he's about to lose control. And when he does, I don't want to be in the firing line." He looked at Siobhan who was sitting beside him, her face pale and drawn." None of us should. You should say something to him, Daniel. You're about the same age, he might listen to you."

"Me? Yeah, no thanks. You want me to get shot? Look at him, he's definitely not stable. You wouldn't know what could push him over the edge. Let Sadie try. She seems to get on better with him."

"Well, we have to do something," Siobhan insisted. "We can't just sit around and wait for something to happen. There's four of us and only one of him. Maybe we can overpower him, get the gun."

Daniel shook his head, not liking the sound of that at all. "And what if something goes wrong? What happens if we try and rush him, and that other guy comes back? Or the guards storm the place and we're caught in the middle?"

There must have been more movement outside because JJ sprinted across the room to the front door and opened it just wide enough to shout out.

"Don't come a step closer," he roared, spittle flying. "I'm warning you, if you don't move back now then one of these hostages is getting a bullet in the head, understand?"

He slammed the door and retreated back into the library. Evidently, whoever was outside had heeded his warning; there was no sign of any armed gardaí storming the building.

Maxwell looked at Daniel and shrugged his shoulders. "Talk to him," he mouthed. "Maybe he'll see sense."

Daniel didn't think JJ was in the mood for seeing sense, but the pain in his head and his ankle had left him a little short-tempered and annoyed, and he was always a little braver when he felt annoyed. He swallowed, and opened his mouth to speak, his heart thumping wildly. For a moment, he couldn't find the words to speak, and he was back in school again, standing in front of his tormenters, trying and failing to stand up for himself, to tell them to back off and leave him alone. His palms had been sweating then too, his cheeks flushed, heart beating as he dug deep to find courage. He cleared his throat.

"Don't you think you should try and negotiate with them?" he said, his voice a little croaky from fear and lack of use. "The gardaí? There's probably some way this can all be fixed."

JJ said nothing, keeping his back to them. Perhaps he hadn't heard. Daniel tried again, his voice a little louder.

"Nobody has to get hurt. We – we could say you treated us well."

JJ whirled, anger flashing across his face. "What did you say?" He marched over and pointed the gun point blank in Daniel's face. He could hear Siobhan's gasp close by and could sense Maxwell slowly edging away. Sadie's face was chalk white.

Daniel fell silent, raising his hands, then suddenly dived at JJ, punching at his injured leg. Pain coursed through Daniel as he grappled with JJ on the ground, their attacker turning this way and that as he tried to shake him off. Maxwell came to his aid, trying to grab hold of the gun, but JJ lashed out with a vicious punch and Maxwell shrieked, rolling away as he clutched his bleeding nose.

Fighting, Daniel quickly realised, is nothing like how it looks in films. In reality, it's vicious and draining. There's no taunting, no clever quips or monologues, just blocking the next strike and trying to land your own. One way or another, this would be over quickly. Daniel thought he was relatively fit, especially considering he went to the gym twice a week, but after barely a minute he was panting as though he'd run a few miles, sweat pouring from his face, his heart pounding furiously.

He gasped as JJ landed a punch on his ribs and suddenly the other man's arms were around his neck, and he was choking. His arms scrabbled to try and free himself, but he could already feel himself getting light-headed and fear flooded through him. And then the grip loosened as JJ roared; Siobhan had run up and kicked him as hard as she could in the back, then dragged Daniel away from him.

Daniel staggered to his feet, clutching his ribs and wincing as pain shot through his chest and his injured leg. When he straightened, JJ was pointing a gun at Siobhan.

"Don't shoot," he pleaded. "I'm sorry, I won't say another word. I'm sorry."

JJ's face was full of contempt, and he spat at Daniel, a globule of saliva landing in his hair.

"You think I need your help?" JJ half-shouted, his face contorted in anger. "I'll get out of this on my own, don't you worry about that."

He glanced at Sadie, grinned, and then in a flash was by her side, dragging her to her feet, the gun pointed to her head.

"Nobody move," he hissed, a trickle of blood running down his forehead. "Or I'll shoot her." His grip tightened on the gun. "I've had it up to here with the lot of ye. All ye had to do was sit tight, keep quiet, just for a little while, and this all could have been sorted without any fuss. But no. You all had to stick your oar in and look where we are now. Up to our necks."

There was a manic look in JJ's eyes, and a cold shiver ran down Daniel's spine as he realised the man was losing the plot and was liable to do anything. And young brave Sadie was right in the firing line. Without thinking, Daniel was standing, then running towards Sadie in a frantic attempt to save her. The next five seconds slowed to a crawl. He watched as JJ's hand moved the gun away from Sadie and pointed it directly towards him.

There was a loud bang and Daniel felt as though someone had punched him, hard, in the chest, and he staggered to a halt. The world began to tilt, colour draining away from the corners of his vision.

As he fell to the ground, he saw Maxwell running at JJ, wrestling him for the gun. Then the nearby door burst open, a sea of uniforms flooding into the building, and everything went to black.

Chapter 61

DCI Barry watched intently as DCI Darcy took the call. Suddenly he leapt and punched the air, "They got him."

"Unbelievable," DCI Barry exhaled. "What next? Those two still have hostages in there."

DCI Darcy called his men around him.

"We go ahead with the plan."

DCI Barry walked off to go and update the superintendent, he sat in his car and made sure all his windows were closed before making the call. After about five rings the superintendent picked up.

"What's the situation lad?" he bellowed into the phone.

"Hi sir, so the situation is we have two armed suspects, firearms are going to surround the building and then cause a distraction to enable them to breach. They are just starting to take up positions now so I must go, I'll call as soon as I have an update."

With that, Barry got out of his squad car and walked over to Darcy and gave him the nod.

"Ok all teams go," he said with authority into the radio.

All members of the team that were set to breach the door moved with military precision in a single file and then spread out either side of the perimeter.

The lead officer took out a flashbang grenade and threw it in the window. There was a ferocious bang, and the team broke down the door of the library rushing in with their guns drawn in all directions. They moved in pairs swiftly clearing the first area of the library. They then broke off into two teams for the back of the library, one team going left and one going right.

"Armed police. Armed police. Drop your weapons." Multiple shouts from the team filled the air mingled with the cries from the hostages.

"Don't shoot, don't shoot."

Maxwell dropped to his knees, his hands up over his head. JJ grabbed a distraught Sadie and held her in front of him as a human shield.

"What are you doing?" Sadie screamed. "JJ, please, let me go. It's over."

JJ had his left arm firmly around her with the gun pointed towards her head.

"Nobody move or I'll blow her head off," he said with venom at the team of officers whose guns were trained in his direction.

"Ok, we aren't going to do anything, we just want to talk if that's ok," said the lead officer.

"Well, what if I don't want to talk," JJ said, his eyes flying in all directions.

"Look, we just want everyone to go home unharmed," the firearms supervisor said in a calm, even tone.

JJ edged towards the door behind him with his hostage while still keeping his eyes on all the officers in front of him. He opened the door with his foot, without loosening his grip on the Sadie or the gun. Before the team could react, in one swift movement he pushed Sadie away from him, stepped through the fire door and slammed it shut behind him. The sound of a dead bolt echoed through the library.

Within seconds tension evaporated as the team moved to help the hostages.

"Clear," Sergeant Daly lifted his radio, "Four hostages, repeat four hostages, two female, two male. Medical assistance required. One hostile, escaped to rear, armed."

Brendan the friendly medic from earlier arrived in seconds, followed by two others.

"Help Daniel, please. He's been shot."

Daniel was unconscious but alive. The bullet had gone straight through, narrowly missing his vital organs. He had lost a lot of blood, but he would survive. Maxwell refused to leave until he was sure that Daniel was going to live. When Daniel was put into the first ambulance, Maxwell went into the second and both went to hospital.

"We're missing two hostages," Sadie said between sobs. "Olive is down in the basement. JJ hit her so hard. She might be dead. She wasn't moving when we left her."

"Is that where the hostile is gone?" Sergeant Daly asked.

"He could be."

Siobhan put her arms around a distraught Sadie as the Garda team huddled together and discussed tactics. The sound of the deadbolt on the far side of the fire door dragging slowly across silenced everyone. Sergeant Daly and his men trained their weapons on the door as it opened little by little.

Olive's voice sounded out, "Don't shoot, gentlemen."

Sadie gave a gasp of relief and ran forward. The door opened fully to reveal Betty supporting an upbeat but battered looking Olive. Her clothes were dishevelled, her hair matted with dried blood, and she was deathly pale.

"He's in there," Betty gestured behind her. "He was no match for Olive."

The medics raced forward and brought the Betty and Olive to one side for treatment while the Garda stepped into the corridor. A few meters away, JJ was cable tied to the handrail, trembling with rage.

"Keep that mad cow away from me," he shouted.

The burly Garda laughed at the sight of him. "What, that little old lady beat you up. Some tough guy you are."

Chapter 62

"Mom, do you think we should cancel the party?" Georgina tentatively asked, aware that Miriam was in a very emotional state. Miriam still hadn't heard from Ciaran and her son Pete was trying, without any luck so far, to get through to Newbridge Garda Station.

"Cancel? Do you think we should? Yes, I suppose it would be best with everything going on. What do you think we should do, Georgie? I just can't think straight. I just wish your dad would phone and let me know he's OK."

A cup of coffee that Georgina had handed her mother ages ago lay untouched on the bedroom windowsill as Miriam stood by the window, her eyes peeled in the hope that Ciaran's car would pull into the drive. She checked her phone constantly only to return it to her dressing gown pocket despondently. Tracey and Pete joined their mother and sister having had a chat in the kitchen about how the evening was unfolding. They were worried about their father, naturally, but a decision was needed about the planned 30th anniversary party.

"Time is marching on, mom, and even if dad comes home now, I reckon he'll be exhausted and stressed by what happened in Newbridge today. We think a party is the last thing he'd want," said Pete. "I think we should postpone the party for the moment, but we need to make a decision one way or the other."

"Postpone rather than cancel, mom," said Tracey putting the emphasis on postpone as she put her arms around her mom and looked into her eyes. "But it's your party, mom. You have to make the decision."

Miriam hesitated momentarily. She couldn't think straight at the moment, but she knew what the kids were saying made sense.

"Go on, do it - postpone it. Do whatever you need to do. Georgie, what about the caterers? And all that food? You put so much work into it, you all did."

"Leave it to us, mom. Just try to relax. I'm sure if anything had happened to Dad you would have heard from the station."

Within minutes Miriam's phone rang. In her haste to get it out of her pocket she almost dropped it, her hands shook so much. 'Thank God, it's Ciaran,' she whispered as she put the phone to her ear. He was OK.

A week later Miriam knew she was in for a long morning waiting, yet again, for another phone call from Ciaran. He had been called in by his superiors, including the Commissioner, to recount exactly what happened in Newbridge library on Derby Day. He had given his account verbally and in writing and today there would be further questioning and probing by the top brass.

Nobody was more critical than Darcy himself of the fact that he hadn't got an inkling that there was a mole operating right under his nose. Night after night he had lain awake scouring through the last few months looking for any shred of evidence that should have alerted him to Tom Moore's treachery. He could find none.

Was he himself culpable because he trusted Moore? Would it look as if he was in cahoots with him? This was a big worry for him, although he had been told that Moore confessed to everything and said he had worked alone. It started out with small bits of intelligence passed on for back-handers, but greed got the better of him, the bloody eejit. What haunted Darcy most was the betrayal of one of his trusted staff who was feeding sensitive information to a notorious drug gang. It reflected very badly on the Gardai that one of its own was now in prison awaiting trial. The papers were having a field day.

"I could be reprimanded for not being on top of the job or worse," he worriedly told Miriam before he left the house for the meeting. "Although, to be honest, even though I've been dreading this day I'll be glad to have it over and done with."

"Ciaran, you've earned yourself a brilliant reputation since the day you joined the guards and you're going to be fine. That little scumbag was very clever, hiding behind his wife's money. You've nothing to be ashamed of. I've always been and always will be, very proud of you." she said as she hugged him in the hallway.

"I'll phone you as soon as I can," he said, kissing her on the cheek. He straightened his shoulders and opened the hall door.

Miriam knew how important Ciaran's record in the Gardai was to him. If she was to sum up Ciaran in one word, it would be integrity. There was never a doubt in her mind that he would always do the right thing. She hoped that his superiors would see it that way, but you never knew. If they were looking for a scapegoat... no, she couldn't let her mind go there. She needed to keep busy this morning to take her mind off that meeting, so she headed up the stairs to wake Georgina and start planning for the weekend.

Georgina was heading back to Australia next week and had rearranged the party for the coming Saturday, three days away. It would be a good chance for her to catch up with family and friends and, Miriam hoped, Ciaran could put all this business of the library hold-up behind him.

The garden looked amazing as dusk approached on Saturday night with lights and lanterns casting a warm, magical air as guests tucked in to their delayed celebratory supper. Ciaran and Miriam were relieved that the harrowing week was over, and they could finally relax with family and friends.

The Commissioner had thanked Ciaran for his management of the hostage situation in the library, in particular for keeping each member of the writing group alive in such a volatile situation. It was acknowledged that Moore was a 'devious bugger' who would be dealt with harshly in court.

Chapter 63

"Good to see you Olive," Ciaran Darcy kissed Olive's cheek.

"You too, Ciaran, although not as happy as I was to see you last Saturday."

"You couldn't help yourself, could you?"

"In fairness, Ciaran. That JJ is a right eejit."

Ciaran gestured towards Olive's face. The expensive makeup nearly disguised the bruising but not quite. She had explained away her slight limp to the other guests as a sports injury, but Ciaran knew better.

"You should've tackled him."

"We didn't. We just let him follow us. He saw us go into that storeroom and followed us thinking he would take us hostage, again. Siobhan had left that outer door open. He ran through it thinking we were out there. We locked him out. Simple. Actually, it's Siobhan we have to thank for having the wherewithal to think of leaving that door open."

"If anything had happened to you, I would never have forgiven myself."

"Nonsense. How were you to know I would end up as a hostage in a library of all places."

"It's crazy, isn't it. Thank God everyone got out relatively unscathed."

"What will happen to Larry? I honestly don't believe he's bad. A bit stupid maybe but I don't think there's any badness in him."

"The file has been sent to the DPP. I think they will be easy on him. There were extenuating circumstances. And he has a new baby son to look after. His employer is a good sort. When he heard the full story, he offered Larry his job back."

"I'm surprised by that. But having said that, he did try to keep his employer's money safe. And he did give you the information you needed to arrest The Carpenter."

"That will go in his favour."

"What are you two plotting over here. Saving the world, one library at a time?" John smiled at them. Olive took his arm and kissed his cheek.

"John, your darling brother wouldn't allow me to do anything in the library. I was left twiddling my thumbs and pretending to be an old woman."

"Nothing old about you, my dear. You will outlive and outwit us all."

Georgina Darcy held out a tray with full champagne glasses.

"Come on, you lot. It's a party. Show the younger generation how it's done."

Miriam Darcy smiled at her daughter before clinking glasses with her favourite sister-in-law. Her brother John was a lucky man to have married such a wonderful woman. It was great to see them enjoying their retirement together. They both had high powered jobs in the city, although to this day she had no idea what Olive's job description had been.

Chapter 64

Muffled sounds seeped through Maxwell's brain - a distant phone ringing, the thud of a door closing, delph clinking, voices he couldn't identify speaking in different languages. Then nothing. Oblivion. Sometime later, he had no idea how long, he was roused from the depths by a cool hand wrapping something around his left upper arm and a woman's soothing voice.

"Hello there. Welcome back to the world. Can you tell me your name and date of birth?"

He hardly recognised his own voice as he responded weakly, "Maxwell Wright, 30th July 1954."

"Good man. You're back from surgery, Maxwell, and it went very well. You'll have a lovely new nose when the swelling goes down in a few days and your facial bruising heals. Just don't look in the mirror or you might get a fright! I'm checking your blood pressure and making sure you're comfortable. You've been through quite an ordeal but you're going to be good as new in no time."

Maxwell was safe at last. He sighed and lay back on his propped-up pillows, relief flooding over him as he glanced around the hospital room. Snapshots of memories flickered before his eyes, scary, painful memories. The relief of finally getting out of the library alive and of knowing that everyone in the writers group survived was like a soothing balm calming him.

"Here you go, hon. A nice cuppa tea and some toast. There's nothing like it when you're under the weather. Give me a shout if you need anything else." A youngish woman in a bright blue overall and cap set a tray on the revolving table at his bedside and spun it around so he could reach it easily.

"Thank you, it's just what I need," said Maxwell.

After the tea he drifted off to sleep and woke again to his wrist being held by the same nurse. She seemed happy with his pulse rate and gave him some painkillers and water. They chatted for a few minutes about the recovery process and possible discharge dates. There was one particular question Maxwell was curious about.

"A young man was admitted at the same time as me. Daniel is his name. Would you know how he's doing? He's in the writer's group and he had pretty severe injuries. Would you be able to find out for me?"

The nurse nodded. "I know the chap you're talking about and he's just back from surgery now. He's doing OK but I'll tell him you were enquiring about him when he wakes up. Now, you just concentrate on yourself and rest. You need lots of rest."

And rest is what he had, drifting in and out of sleep for the next two days. Occasionally he was told that one of the writers phoned to see how he was doing. Early on the third day he sussed out where Daniel was and made his way to see him. Despite his injuries he was as chipper as always.

"I thought it was a bit of an adventure at first, but it all got out of hand," admitted Daniel. "Look at us now, man. You look like a bus ran over your face and I look like I crashed the bus into a wall. You know, I really am sorry about the diary. I was only messin' but my mum is right, she's always at me to 'cut out that messing or you'll land yourself in trouble."

Maxwell couldn't help but smile and said he accepted the apology. They chatted for a while, and he told Daniel that in some ways he was glad that the truth was out. He was sick and tired pretending everything was OK when it wasn't. "Maybe you did me a favour, Daniel, even if I didn't feel like that at the time."

Maxwell wound his way back to his ward and sat on a chair beside the bed. He was starting to feel more like himself yet, despite that, he was anxious about going home the following day. He felt more alone than ever. As he pondered on his release from hospital, he decided he'd take one of the taxis outside the main entrance and stop at his local shop for a few groceries. Then he heard a short tap on the door. 'Come in', he called, and a head popped around the door – a young curly headed blonde girl, about four he reckoned, shyly peeped in and then disappeared. The door opened wider and to Maxwell's astonishment his son Ciaran was standing in the doorway holding the little girl's hand.

"OK to come in, dad? Grainne here wants to meet her grandfather, don't you love?" The child nodded vigorously, her curls bouncing around. She let go of her dad's hand mad and made her way over towards Maxwell, staring intently at him. "Oh, your face is all bandaged up. Is it sore? Are you getting a new nose? My dad saw you on the tele being wheeled into the ambulance and that's why we came to see you."

Maxwell couldn't believe it. In all the confusion and relief of being released from the library he hadn't taken much notice of the swell of media. It never occurred to him that the cameras caught him. He looked over at Ciaran who smiled broadly at him.

"We've a lot to catch up with, dad. I was looking for you for a while but not that hard really, I have to admit. When I saw you on the news, I couldn't believe my eyes. In fact, I wasn't sure it was you because your face was so bloody and swollen so I phoned the Gardai to check and here we are."

Maxwell felt like crying but managed to pull himself together.

"Yes, we've a lot to catch up with but I'm glad you're here, Ciaran, and I'm so happy to meet you Grainne. To answer your questions, I'm getting my nose fixed and it's a little bit sore but not too bad. And now that you're here I couldn't be happier."

The little girl made her way over to where Maxwell sat and reached out for a hug. It was the best moment of his life.

Chapter 65

Ciaran insisted that he would collect his dad from hospital and bring him to his house for a few days to help get his strength back.

"Aisling suggested it, dad, and of course Grainne is telling all her friends that her grandad is coming. I think she has them all lined up to visit her prize exhibit – your new nose. And the fact that you were on TV is a huge draw. You're quite the celebrity in her eyes."

"Maybe I should just go home, Ciaran. I'm not sure I'm up to all this fuss and talking to people yet. I think I just need to be on my own for a while, you know, to sort things out in my head. But I want you to know that I'm very glad you came – and brought Grainne of course." He choked up a bit, so Ciaran reached over to where his father was seated beside him and patted his hand.

"Dad, there's no pressure but a few days rest might be better for you than going home to an empty flat. Let's give it a try and if you're not comfortable I'll drop you home. What do you say?"

The last few days had been harrowing for Maxwell. His cover-up of his past had been blown wide open leaving him vulnerable and a bit shaky. He was only coming to terms with the reunion with Ciaran after all this time. Too much was happening too quickly. On the other hand, he knew it was his chance, perhaps his only chance, to reconnect with his family.

Maxwell sighed, "Well, OK. I don't want to get in the way, but it would be great to see Grainne again, and catch up with you and Aisling."

It wasn't a long drive to Ciaran's, about 30 minutes. "Still playing the GAA or is it golf now?" asked Maxwell, sticking firming to the safe ground of sport.

"Junior B team is my level now, dad. Just the odd game of golf and Aisling joined the tennis club last year so between everything we're kept pretty busy."

Nothing as personal as feelings came into the conversation, much to the relief of father and son.

The house was quiet with Aisling at work and Grainne at playschool. Ciaran showed Maxwell to the spare room and went into the kitchen, flicking on the kettle and setting two mugs on the table. He was humming away to himself. The previous night Ciaran had done a lot of soul searching, prompted by Aisling.

"How are you feeling about your dad now, Ciaran?" she asked when she had settled Grainne in bed. She handed Ciaran a beer and cosied up beside him, as she sipped a glass of red wine. "I know you were angry with him over the years but now that you've seen him do you think you've forgiven him?"

"Forgiven him? Yea, I suppose so. As a kid I was so proud of him, I wanted to be like him, to be looked up to and respected. When he let us down, I wanted to punish him. It was so public in all the papers and so humiliating. My college friends didn't know what to say to me, so they just avoided me. I was so angry that all I wanted to do was to just shut him out of my life. I never wanted to have anything to do with him again."

"And what about now?" asked Aisling.

Ciaran glugged from his bottle of beer and didn't respond immediately. He had hardly recognised the old man sitting beside the hospital bed and it was Grainne who rescued the situation.

"When I saw him today it broke my heart, Ash. He looked so fragile and vulnerable. I realised I was wrong to let it get this far. I guess I'm to blame for being so harsh, to have shut him out for so long. He's my dad, Grainne's grandad."

They talked well into the night and Ciaran made up his mind that over the next few days he would try to rekindle the relationship. As Ash had said 'we all make mistakes, it's life, but maybe it's time to move on.' His dad was upstairs now in a house he had never seen. He hoped he'd be a regular visitor from now on.

Ciaran set the coffee pot on the table and a plate of fancy cakes Aisling had left for them. He ambled into the hall and called his dad. No response. He raised his voice a little. "Dad, your coffee's ready."

Still no response. He ran up the stairs, tapped on the bedroom door and quickly opened it sensing something was wrong. Maxwell was lying on the floor, unconscious. Shock struck him like a hammer blow, and he ran over, knelt down and checked to see if his father was breathing. It was shallow but he was alive. Hands trembling, he reached for the mobile phone in his pocket and dialled the emergency services.

"I need an ambulance urgently. My dad has collapsed and he's unconscious on the floor. What should I do?" he asked, his voice shaking. He answered all the questions asked and followed instructions over the phone, making sure his father was comfortable before taking two steps at a time on the stairs to unlock the hall door.

Maxwell remained unconscious as the ambulance raced to the hospital followed closely by Ciaran. He knew his father was in a critical condition, that it was touch and go. His heart had stopped before they left the house and the medics had got him back again. 'Please God, let him survive,' Ciaran whispered repeatedly. He hadn't been in touch with God for decades but hoped he or she wouldn't hold it against him now. His mind raced. He needed to get hold of his sister, Saoirse, and let her know what had happened. She wasn't even aware that he had been in touch with his dad. He had decided to wait until he saw the lay of the land before he told her he had met him. It was too late now for that.

"Saoirse, I'm afraid it's bad news."

Chapter 66

The small church filled up gradually as the organist played soothing music, familiar to many of the congregation as it formed a backdrop to whispered conversations.

Friends of Saoirse, grouped together midway up the church, spoke in hushed tones.

"Wasn't it incredible the way Ciaran spotted his dad on the telly and then it led to him meeting him again."

"Seemingly the Gardai told Ciaran and Saoirse that their dad approached one of the hostage takers and pleaded with him to take him and let the others go. He was prepared to put his life on the line for the rest of the writing group. Brave man."

"I know there was some incident in his past where he regretted not taking the right action – something to do with work - and that was why he became alienated from the family."

"The whole hostage thing was incredible. You'd never in your wildest dreams expect that sort of thing to happen in a library. Saoirse and Ciaran met one of them since and they seem like an extraordinary bunch of people. Saoirse told me some of them are coming to the church today to show their support for Maxwell."

Suddenly, the tempo of the music changed, and a hush came over the congregation. Heads turned around as Saoirse entered the church resplendent in her wedding gown, her arm linked with Maxwell's.

"This is the best day of my life, dad, and I'm so glad to have you here," she said. Maxwell bent down and kissed her on the cheek.

"Me too," he whispered, and they made their way slowly up the aisle.

Chapter 67

The Carpenter lay motionless in the dark, hands behind his head, staring at the underside of the top bunk. The tiny room was quiet, the silence punctuated at intervals by a grunt or rustle from his cellmate above. The first night, he knew from experience, was often the most difficult, the cold realisation setting in that these four walls would become your world for weeks, months, even years. Stripped of your humanity, segregated from the world beyond the prison gates. Life reduced to a repetitive timetable, someone else in charge of your waking and sleeping moments. The need to be constantly alert was exhausting – a man in his position would be a target from rival gang members looking to make a name for themselves or settle old scores.

He sighed, turning this way and that, trying to get comfortable on the thin prison-issue mattress, then sat up and swung his legs out and onto the ground. The sounds of a prison at night were both familiar and strange; faint cries from inmates talking in their sleep, low muttering from one or two cells nearby, the click-clack of a guard's shoes as they did their rounds.

The Carpenter had done several stretches inside; two months just after his 18th birthday for his third criminal damage conviction, six months a year later when he was caught selling drugs yet again, a month here and there for theft and public order and offences he couldn't even remember. Water under the bridge by this stage; he'd quickly graduated to a much higher class of criminality.

He'd told a judge once he could do a year standing on his head, no problem, and it was true. Eleven years, though. That was a different story. He could run his empire from the inside without too much trouble – all you needed was a phone – but he knew not being out there in person would test the foundations of what he'd built. Already, there were whispers, murmurs of the world moving on without him. The Carpenter had plenty of enemies, even within his own ranks, he knew. They wouldn't waste any time.

He closed his eyes, thoughts of the Caribbean and what might have been briefly floating through his mind until he dispelled them with a shake of his head. That sort of thinking, he knew, would only make the coming years ten times harder.

He shook his head, a bitter smile spreading across his lips as he wondered for the millionth time how things had come to this. The best-laid plan, scuppered by incompetence and disloyalty. And, as the trial had heard, the efforts of a rag-tag group of writers in that damned library, ordinary, talentless morons who had somehow managed to drive a wedge between their kidnappers and set off a chain reaction that disrupted all his plans and dreams.

Perhaps, he thought, in the distant future when his sentence was served and he could step foot in the outside world once more, he would pay a little visit to Newbridge and meet them for himself.

THE END – OR IS IT?

Acknowledgements

This book was a joint effort between the members of the Ink Tank Creative Writing Group based in Newbridge Library.

The idea was first mooted by Diarmuid Farrelly and after much discussion the others came on board. Each person wrote a chapter following on from the next so no one knew what would happen next. Some writers fell for certain characters and wrote their chapters, others concentrated on the storyline. We lost a couple of characters along the way and the final outcome changed several times. The editing and final tying up of loose ends was a logistical nightmare but we got there. We hope you, our readers, enjoy reading our story as much as we all enjoyed writing it.

Contributors in no particular order

Diarmuid Farrelly, Maria McDonald, Kay Kevlihan,

Helen McGlynn, Conor Forrest, Tara Phelan, Daniel Riordan

Editors in no particular order

Breda Reid, Eleanor Wauchob, Martin Condon

Our book cover was designed by Paul McDonald of Mac Designs. You can follow his designs on Instagram @mac_designco

We would like to thank sincerely the staff of Newbridge Library for their unwavering support of our writers' group. We would also like to thank Kildare County Council for granting us the Local publishing Award which enabled us to cover the costs of printing and allowed us to donate the proceeds to charity.

Our chosen charity is the Samaritans. Please support their amazing work in our community.

Printed in Great Britain
by Amazon